I0534589

UNHEROIC: BOOK THREE

© 2021 Marcus V. Calvert

By Tales Unlimited, LLC.

All rights reserved.

No portion of this book may be reproduced in any form without permission from the publisher.

For permissions, contact: www.talesunlimited.net

Cover by Lincoln Adams

ACKNOWLEDGMENTS

I'd like to thank Lincoln Adams (my long-time cover artist) for his time, patience, and wicked-awesome skill.

Rose, thanks for keeping me in the game.

To my editor and beta readers, thanks for your irritating eye(s) for detail.

To everyone else who had a hand in this twisted thing being written (living or not), I thank you.

I must also tip a hat to my fellow artists and strangers-turned-fans. You truly are a hip crowd.

Contents

7 · Unheroic: Book Three

A SILLY IDEA

Being a demon in New Mexico was like an indefinite trip to the spa. Aside from holy ground and exorcists, not much could hurt me. I was an alpha predator in a world full of tasty sheep. While I had to sweat the occasional foe, most weren't bulletproof.

When I first came here, I possessed Emmet Salzin: asshole biker. The divorced sex addict was easy pickings with a decent stash of dirty money at his disposal. Once I ate the poor bastard's soul, Emmet's memories became mine: including his habits, fears, and working knowledge of the Chrome Eagles.

Essentially, I knew the man well enough to become him.

The Chrome Eagles were a fun little crew. A few years back, the founding members split off from three other biker gangs to form their own. They specialized in gunrunning and designer drugs. Odds were that the feds were currently building a case on 'em. By the time that happened, I'd be long gone.

Most demons would've taken over the outfit (and the many headaches that came with it). Nah. One of the many things Hell taught me was to never run shit. Nope, true power came from being the fifth or so guy in line— but with the boss' ear.

Do it right and there were fewer chores to sweat and even fewer betrayals. Being a founding member of the Chrome Eagles, Emmet was a good soldier and confidante. That made him the perfect choice when I left Hell.

Why'd I end up on the mortal plane? Market forces were against me. With the surprising ratio of souls going into the Pit, the bigwigs had to rely more and more on automation.

There just weren't enough of us demons to process the inflow of newly damned. The tech got better and better, until the inevitable happened: *fucking layoffs.* Never in the history of Hell were demons downsized in such numbers.

Whose idea was it? Mine.

It only took me two generations to funnel it up through tiers of glory hound demon types. When the Big Man heard it, he stole the idea and went after us mid-level demons. We were overpaid and underskilled (especially on the corporate side). Replacing us with AI mainframes made way too much sense.

Most demons opted for unemployment, which wouldn't expire for a half-eon or until Judgment Day (whichever came first). There was a second option, which few demons even considered: retirement. Those who went that route received a diddly pension and a gold watch.

It didn't surprise me that so few of my brothers and sisters lacked the grit to retire. We demons were as addicted to Hell as our haloed counterparts were to Heaven. The servants of either side felt out of place anywhere else. I wonder how people would've reacted if they knew that angels and demons could freely roam the mortal world whenever they wanted.

Hell had its moments. Yes, the drinks were cheap and there were plenty of unique delights. Too bad the predictability of it all left me a bit numb inside. That's why I decided to stray into mankind's backyard and seek out new challenges to enjoy.

If Hell's unnatural allure reeled me back, so be it. Yet, with modern civilization's many diversions, I didn't expect to be bored anytime soon. I planned to stay in Emmet's body for a few more months then move on. I wanted to leave my demonic fingerprints all over this twisted little world, until the End Times.

There was another motivation behind my choice. Ever since the Messiah, it was way too easy to get through the Pearly Gates. Baptism, routine worship, or even belief in God were strictly optional now. One simply had to avoid violating the serious Commandments and rack up enough good deeds. It never ceased to amaze how many mortals missed their shot at Heaven by only a few kind acts.

That's why I sought to help mortals blithely toss away their easy chances at Paradise. People played dumb (but they understood). Money wasn't the root of all evil—*desire was.*

All one had to do was push the right buttons and watch mortals damn themselves to get their heart's desire. The "motive" didn't matter as much as which sins got done: from white lies to murder. In a mortal world full of fads and wonders, new sins would pop up until the Apocalypse.

When that "special day" came, we'd win, of course.

For all their bluster, Heaven was outgunned and they knew it. Naturally, God could tip the scales . . . except He won't. Ever since His only son got crucified (which wasn't part of the Plan), the Big G's been sulking.

He's expected to sit out the final battle, simply because humans weren't worth saving—even the apple polishers who truly earned Paradise. Of course, righteous mortals would freak if they knew this. Maybe if they paid more attention to the Old Testament version of the Almighty, they'd understand His mood swings.

Whether or not Heaven burns, Earth is destined to roast in the crossfire. Then again, the human race might surprise both sides and become extinct ahead of schedule. Wouldn't that be funny? Either way, what self-respecting demon wouldn't want a front-row seat to this world's slow-motion doomsday?

The inevitability of it all gave me a woody as I rolled down a dirt road toward Crunky's Roadhouse. Shitty name aside, they made a worthy steak and the booze wasn't too watered down. I parked next to a row of bikes, all tricked out with Chrome Eagles' colors.

Under the beating heat of an August sky, I headed toward the front door. Music was pumping and (this time of day) there should've been a lady or two in the house. Since I resided in the body of a sex addict, I'd be sure to bring one home with me.

Then I noticed a collective stench: the aroma of freshly killed bodies and the scent of cordite. Without slowing my stride, I entered the bar and took in the carnage. Eleven dead men and women littered the place. Even the staff got wasted.

Broken small arms and spent brass littered the floor. Aside from myself, there was only one other dog in this yard—and this one had a halo. The smug angel waited in the center of the room. His mortal host was a middle-aged male Latino in his mid-forties.

The angel's host body was smaller than mine and sported the silvery halo of a warrior chump. His was the kind Heaven would dump on the front lines to die in the war to come. He wore a black suit, white shirt, and yellow tie—all without a wrinkle or spec of blood. Even his black Gucci loafers gleamed. The fucker looked like a damned suit model.

"Usominor!" grinned the angel. "The honor is truly mine!"

I grimly stepped over bodies and shell casings, until there was only a large round table between us. Yeah, I had a Glock. My touch would turn the weapon unholy. A few well-placed shots could kill this angel's host body and send him back to Heaven.

There was just one big hole in this tempting idea. Angels had the same advantage. Even if he wasn't packin', we stood in a roomful of guns (some of which still worked). Physically, we were about a match. Hand-to-hand, a fight could take a few hours to finish.

I gave the murder scene another quick once-over. Everyone in this place looked broken. Yeah, some of them were clipped by stray fire but they were all killed by hand. Whether by a broken neck or torn-off limb, this fucker had no problems with brutality.

I had to respect that.

"How do you angels do it?" I asked.

"What?" frowned the angel.

"Kill people, by hand, without a stain or even a wrinkle?" I replied. "What's the trick?"

The angel shrugged. "One of the perks, Brother Usominor."

I ignored the "Brother" crack and resisted the urge to argue the metaphysics of our relationship. Granted, God created us both as angels. But when He condemned the Fallen, those ties shriveled and died as our halos became horns.

"Speak your mind," I scowled. "Start with your name."

"Call me 'Trevor.'"

I gave the angel a knowing sigh.

True names had power in the wrong hands. If he wanted to, Trevor could whisper mine into some do-gooder's head, along with instructions on how to banish or imprison me. If someone gave me an angels' true name, I would've done much worse with it.

Before the rebellion, I knew every angel in Heaven. When God cast us out, He burned that knowledge from every demon's head but allowed the angels to remember everything about us.

"We were wondering if you were up for some freelance work?" asked the dead-serious angel.

"What are you offering?" I smirked, all but certain this offer was some kind of ruse.

Trevor paused to consider my question.

"Something reasonable, per kill," he explained. "It could be a different favor each time."

"I thought angels did their own killing," I countered, with a nod at the bodies.

Trevor picked up a chair.

"We do," he explained. "Killing sinners isn't a problem with us. I'd like to hire you to kill the innocent."

The angel sat down and gauged my curious reaction. I spotted another gore-splattered chair within easy reach and wiped someone's entrails from it.

"Tell me more," I sighed.

"The Apocalypse isn't that far away—" Trevor began.

"A line that's been used since Christ died," I interrupted.

The warrior angel shook his head while I sat down. "No, Brother. We're about to start some shit."

He waited for that to sink in. I kept the surprise off my face and urged Trevor to continue.

"Obviously, we'd lose in a straight-up conflict, so we've had to think outside of the box."

"What about God?" I asked.

"Father's sitting this one out," Trevor confirmed. "However, He's allowed us to abandon the ancient rules of conduct."

"You're sinking to our level?" I grinned, genuinely intrigued.

Trevor cautiously nodded. Assuming it wasn't bullshit, this intel would've been priceless Downstairs.

"And one of these strategies is to kill the innocent?" I asked.

Trevor nodded. "Now guess why."

"That part's obvious," I scoffed. "Killing enough people, before they damn themselves, would send more of them your way. With enough time, Heaven could triple its soul ranks."

"Still think we'd lose?" asked the angel.

I nodded with a mocking sigh.

"You bastards have no head for 'big picture' evil," I explained. "When it comes to souls, you've been lagging behind Hell since before humans discovered fire. You fighting us would be like . . . Delaware fighting all of Asia."

The anxious angel willed a lit cigarette into his mouth and thoughtfully took a drag. Then he eyed me with a hint of embarrassment.

"Forgive my manners," sighed Trevor. "Care for a smoke?"

I declined with a polite shake of my head.

"What if we killed the right people?" posed Trevor. "Sinners capable of infecting countless other souls with their evil?"

"Like popping Hitler, back when he was a nobody?" I asked.

"Exactly," he replied.

"Folks would notice Downstairs," I warned him. "Including the Boss."

"Afraid he'd get mad?" Trevor asked through a plume of smoke.

"I'm afraid he'd promote me," I chuckled. "This is Hell we're talking about."

"Wow," Trevor sighed as he flicked ashes over a headless woman's corpse. "Then most of my ideas would be 'too little, too late'?"

"Without hurting your feelings—yeah," I told him. "We're well past that now."

Heaven had an interesting conundrum. The angel leaned back into his chair, seemingly bothered by the realities of my logic.

"What would you do?" Trevor asked.

"To what? Win the Apocalypse?" I asked.

"Yeah," Trevor verbally nudged. "I mean, we're just two fellas talkin' here."

This slaughter-based "Q&A" was meant to pull a viable strategy out of me. Normally, I'd tell Trevor to go fuck himself. Here's the problem: I'm a demon. As in pure, "fuck-everybody" evil. Making the Apocalypse last a bit longer might be fun. I tossed around a few dozen options in my head . . .

"My price is simple and comes in three parts," I replied.

Trevor eyed me with veiled hope in his host's baby browns. "I'm all ears."

"First, you don't start the Apocalypse until I allow you to."

Heaven was predestined to start the final fight. The idea of letting me ring the starting bell put a frown on the angel's face. I expected Trevor to refuse—

"Seems fair," the angel replied.

Wow. They were desperate.

"Second, whenever I'm on the mortal coil, bad karma just rolls off me," I demanded. "Keep things challenging—fun, even—but I can't lose. Ever."

Trevor frowned, sensing the many (many) sins I would commit with such blanket good fortune. Yet, the angel nodded, fully aware of how good my hand was.

"It'll expire at the start of the Apocalypse—"

"Which I won't start anytime soon," I interrupted. "The third thing I want is 'diplomatic immunity'—from your side. No matter what I do on this mortal coil, Heaven can't touch me or have me taken out."

Trevor's eyebrows rose with interest.

"You've got yourself a deal," promised the angel, "assuming your tip is worth it."

Craving a cigarette and a drink, I looked my enemy in the eye.

"What's Hell's best advantage?" I asked.

"Numbers," Trevor replied. "You need computers to track them all."

I gave him a clever smirk and waited for him to figure it out.

"So what?" he scoffed. "You want us to sabotage their computers and buy time? We've tried. Their firewalls are too good."

I stood up and pulled a bottle of whiskey from the adjacent table. Deep in thought, I popped the cap and drained a fifth.

"You angels can't do ruthless, can you?" I smirked, as I came up for air. "Too bad the Angel of Death's a myth. He'd understand."

Trevor impatiently slipped the cigarette back into his mouth and waited for me to get to the point.

"You need to get 'biblical,' my haloed cousin," I argued. "To the point where even Father might get jealous."

It took the angel a few more moments to get it. Then it hit him like an orgasm. His jaw dropped and his eyes bulged.

"A pre-emptive strike, against Hell? *Before* the Apocalypse?" Trevor gasped through a perfect smile. "That's unheard of!"

"Because it's against the ancient rules?" I sneered. "The ones He's letting you ignore?"

The angel reacted with a hopeful nod. "How would you do it?"

"Target the soul hordes and flatten them," I advised. "Whether you use archangels, celestial nukes, or both—a successful sneak attack is what you need. Without their hordes, you might have a fair fight on your hands."

"What if they hit us back?" Trevor asked with logical concern.

"Demons can't make a play for the Pearly Gates," I reminded him. "Not until the Apocalypse officially starts."

While Hell was bound by Father's rules, Trevor didn't seem comforted by that logic. With a shrug, I raised the bottle and drained it with ease. We both knew that Hell would (somehow) make us pay. It just wouldn't be through force of arms. That's one of the reasons I demanded the good luck.

I was half-tempted to remind the angel that he could simply bind the souls of every Fallen—but that would be a step too far. Maybe they'd figure that out on their own (or not). Angels were angels, after all. Still, my immunity deal was solid because his side couldn't lie or betray. Those who did were kicked out of Heaven and ended up on our side of the tracks.

"Once you've thinned the infernal herd, you might not even need to have an Apocalypse," I urged.

Trevor wanted to argue that last part. Then he gave me a patronizing smile.

"Perhaps," he replied. "Thank you for your aid."

"Don't thank me. Just keep your word."

Trevor nodded as he stood up and turned to leave.

"And if anyone asks, I didn't help you," I warned him. "We're just talkin' about a silly idea, right?"

The angel reached the door, then turned my way with a mischievous smile.

"I'd love to, Usominor," Trevor replied. "But that would be a lie."

ATLANTIS ARISEN

Six hours ago, the debate on the existence of alien life was settled when a massive starship abruptly appeared over the Mediterranean. The rectangular vessel was just over thirty miles long, eight miles high, and fifteen miles wide. It descended to an altitude of two miles, then hovered over the water. The crimson-hulled vessel's name was etched along its port side, in some variant of ancient Greek.

Expert linguists claimed that it meant: *Atlantis Arisen.*

Naturally, the modern world slipped into a freaked-out frenzy. Nuclear arsenals were activated. Armies mobilized and evacuations began. The media endlessly speculated, while houses of worship filled up with the terrified faithful.

All attempts at radio contact went unanswered. Fighters flew overhead unchallenged. The U.N. debated over possible courses of action. Rather than wait for their decision, the U.S. government took the initiative and sent a quick reaction squad

*　*　*

A gray C-130 Hercules descended through the late evening clouds, escorted by eight F-22 fighter jets. Inside the plane's cargo hold was a black Humvee with a recoilless rifle on a mounted turret. Riding shotgun was Master Sergeant Lloyd Benton. At thirty-eight, the balding soldier wore full tactical gear over a stocky frame. Kentucky-raised, he sported a reddish goatee and intelligent gray eyes which (depending on the situation) could show charm or heartless menace.

He sized up the rest of his men: Urlowe, Messle, Disson, and Clarke. All of them were seasoned operators with impressive records. Geared up and ready, they had their "game faces" on. Benton was happy to have them along, even though this op should've involved a much larger team.

The master sergeant wanted to go in with more squads, geeks from NASA, a diplomatic team, ancient Greek linguists, tons of gear, and maybe a nuke. Instead, they were going in with a week's rations, a lot of spare ammo, and parachutes. Their orders were to gather intel, make contact, and (if feasible) arrange for more traditional forms of diplomacy.

A greener officer might've believed that last part.

Benton, on the other hand, felt like disposable bait. Whether this op was FUBAR or not, their extraction plan didn't go much further than those parachutes. Having worked operations throughout the world, he had faced all sorts of situations—from meet and greets to stand-up firefights. While landing on a massive UFO went well beyond his pay grade, Benton approached it like another day at the office . . .

*　　*　　*

The C-130 came in low over the alien ship's upper hull and executed a "touch-and-go" landing. Rather than come to a halt, its rear ramp slid open before the plane's huge tires even touched the hull. Out raced the Humvee in the opposite direction. The Hercules sped up, closed its ramp, and lifted off.

Disson was at the wheel. Urlowe was up top with the recoilless rifle. Messle and Clarke were in the back. In Benton's lap was a sturdy little touchpad. He pulled up the latest satellite photos and reviewed them again. Three hours ago, a section of the *Atlantis Arisen's* upper hull opened up. Large enough to drive through, it was tagged as a possible point of entry.

"They dropped us dead-on," Benton estimated. "The entrance should still be open."

"Cool," Disson replied as he floored it. "Think it's a welcome mat?"

Benton considered the question for a few seconds, then shook his head.

"It's never that simple," replied the master sergeant.

*   *   *

The entrance led into a massive corridor, some hundreds of feet high and farther than their eyes could see. Eventually, the Humvee reached a three-way intersection. Disson stopped and turned to Benton.

"Which way, boss?" Disson asked.

"It's like we drove up Jack's beanstalk and no one told us," Benton muttered, before he felt multiple impact tremors. The Delta soldiers tensed up, ready to shoot on Benton's order.

"Where's that coming from?" Urlowe tensely asked.

Disson looked in the rearview mirror and slammed his foot on the gas.

"On our six!" he yelled.

As the Humvee sped forward, Urlowe swiveled the recoilless rifle around . . . and froze. Giant, childish hands closed around the Humvee and lifted it off the floor like it was a toy car.

"Shit!" Urlowe yelled. "Where'd he come from?!"

They found themselves in the hands of a giant-sized boy.

Barely five, he had brown hair, blue eyes, and an adorable face. With a giggle, the child raised the Humvee to his eyes and looked inside at them. Disson took his foot off the gas and eyed his C.O.

Benton leaned out of his window and sized up the kid's knee-length white tunic and brown sandals. Ancient attire aside, the boy reminded him of his stepson back home. The little giant asked them something in a language they couldn't understand.

Urlowe waited for the order to fire. If Benton called it, he'd put an explosive round through the kid's right eye. Of course, he didn't expect any of them to survive the fall . . .

"Hold fire," Benton commanded.

"Copy that," Urlowe acknowledged.

More impact tremors could be heard and a woman arrived behind the child. In her mid-twenties, the green-eyed beauty wore a black silken robe, strapped sandals, and a silver circlet around her braided black hair.

"So they make fine-assed women in outer space?" Disson whispered. "Gives a fella hope."

The soldiers tensed as she knelt beside the boy.

"Ampelios," scolded the woman, in fluent Olympian. "You aren't allowed on this level!"

"I just wanted to see their sky," the boy replied, also in Olympian. "Look what I found!"

The woman noticed the Humvee and its human passengers. As the adult alien moved closer, Benton racked his clever brain for the best way to communicate with her. Assuming they could get past the language barrier, he'd just have to remind his men to show poise and respect to these advanced alien visitors. The master sergeant put on his best smile—

"What's your name beautiful?" shouted Disson, who leaned out of the driver's side window and waved at the giantess.

* * *

Her name was Korinna.

She introduced herself—in perfect English—as a priestess of the Olympian god, Poseidon. The spec ops soldiers had all seen enough movies to know that Poseidon was the "mythical" god of the sea. Korinna carried the Humvee in her left palm and held the boy's hand with her right.

Benton and his men patiently waited as she walked Ampelios into a massive elevator. Several floors and turns later, they reached the modest quarters of the boy's parents—both of whom were on duty. The priestess put the boy to bed, then returned to the elevator.

Along the way, they passed other gigantic Olympians. They all wore robes or tunics similar to ancient Greek origin—only of finer quality. The elevator doors slid open and Korinna carried the Humvee inside.

"Which one of you is the leader?" she asked with a modest accent.

Benton's tiny hand wave caught her eye.

"Master Sergeant Lloyd Benton, ma'am," he replied. "It's a pleasure to meet you."

The priestess gently adjusted the Humvee in her hands, until they could talk face-to-face.

"How many are with you?" Korinna asked as the elevator doors slid closed.

"Just us five," Benton replied. "Are all of you this tall?"

"In human terms, I'm only five-foot-two," she explained with a smile. "Trespassers are cursed by our magicks, which is what happened when you crossed our threshold."

"Our apologies, ma'am," replied the master sergeant. "Is this curse reversible?"

"Absolutely," she assured them.

"That's good to know," Benton said with a forced smile.

A holographic array of symbols appeared before her. Korinna hit three of them and the array disappeared. Then the elevator began to descend.

Benton cleared his throat. "May I ask a personal question?"

The priestess nodded.

"With all of this technology, why would you still believe in magic?"

Korinna gave them a patient smile, as if they too were children.

"Because *magic is real*," explained the priestess. "We've integrated it with our technology almost ten thousand of your years ago. I'm surprised that your people haven't done the same."

Something about her choice of words bothered Benton (and he didn't know why). He also noticed a glimmer of pity behind Korinna's eyes. Like she wanted to tell them something else but couldn't. Then she was all politeness again.

"Do any of you have Greek blood?" Korinna asked.

"Not that we're aware of," Benton replied with a friendly shrug. "But we're from America, so who knows?"

"Ah," Korinna replied with a hint of disappointment.

"Where are we headed?" Benton asked.

"Once you've been returned to your normal size, I'll escort you to the bridge," she replied. "I'm sure Admiral Bikonis will be happy to meet such brave warriors as yourselves. Then we'll have a feast, in your honor."

"Sounds good to me," Benton shrugged. "I haven't been to a feast in a long time."

Korinna's face turned serious. "Once the feasting rituals are done, you will be prepared for the Trials."

Benton fought to keep a smile on his grizzled face. "Say what now?"

* * *

The world held its collective breath for three more days.

Just before sunset, the *Atlantis Arisen* began to move. The massive ship headed toward the island of Crete and stopped a half-kilometer over one of its beaches. Chaos erupted as beachgoers found themselves under the ship's shadow. Some fled while others foolishly flocked to the scene.

Several minutes later, a white beam of conical light emerged from the ship and hit the shoreline. Within seconds, the Humvee materialized. When the light ceased, the alien vessel rose into the twilight sky until it disappeared within a harmless implosion of air.

On the beach, crowds of locals flocked to the Humvee and surrounded it. Benton stepped out while Urlowe remained behind the wheel. The rest of his team wasn't with them. Cameras flashed and questions were shouted (in a half-dozen languages) by overeager reporters who just happened to be in the area.

Benton wearily sat atop the hood of the Humvee and fired up a cigar. A gorgeous *BBC* reporter half-dragged her cameraman through the crowd and caught the master sergeant's attention. As she repeatedly begged for a comment, Benton frowned back at Urlowe, who looked equally drained.

After a moment's hesitation, the subordinate merely shrugged. With a deep breath, Benton held out a hand. The reporter handed him her microphone with a triumphant smile.

"This is 'live,' right?" he asked.

"Absolutely," beamed the ambitious redhead. "Worldwide coverage."

"Then you've just killed my career, you walking blonde joke," Benton snapped with a sarcastic smile. The reporter frowned for a moment, then saw his point. The soldier's face would be seen by billions before tomorrow. For someone who worked spec ops, that just wouldn't do.

Benton was planning to retire soon anyway. Maybe he could wrangle a book deal out of this . . . Nah. The true details of this mess would never see the light of day. The master sergeant hopped off the Humvee, gently shoved the reporter aside, and got in front of the camera.

"I can't give you the full score," Benton announced. "Basically, it comes down to this: they came in peace and they left the same way."

Urlowe involuntarily shuddered as his mind replayed the memory of Messle's death. The first to die during the Trials, he got separated from the team as they eluded centaur archers in the ship's vast hunting grounds. Eventually, they found Messle's arrow-riddled corpse—and those of four centaurs he took with him.

"Thousands of years ago, the ship's leader and his crew crashed on this world," lied Benton. "His two brothers died early on. One he buried on a mountaintop.

The other, in an underground cavern. Eventually, the survivors were rescued—but not before they left a lasting mark upon our world."

The master sergeant paused with a solemn sigh.

"On his deathbed, that same leader chose to spend his final days here—where he could honor his brothers and departed comrades," Benton explained. "Also, he wanted to see what became of us."

The whole crowd waited in silence for the "verdict."

"He was pleasantly surprised," Benton said, through a bullshit smile. "We swapped stories, histories, and three of my men decided to stick around."

Urlowe then thought of Clarke, who ended up in the left-handed grip of a cyclops, about to become a light snack. The one-eyed carnivore must've been seventy feet high. The naked monster stumbled across them during the middle of the hunt. By then, they burned most of their ammo on satyrs, harpies, a gullible gorgon, and a berserk minotaur.

Once it had their scent, the Cyclops was relentless. Dropping the giant beast would've been hopeless, had it not been for Clarke, who armed his last brick of C-4. He tucked it into a pocket, just before the monster cornered him.

The others tried to save him but their shots flattened against the giant's skin. Even its massive eye was bulletproof. Right before the Cyclops could proceed to eat Clarke alive, the doomed soldier set off the brick . . .

"Why did the rest of your men stay?" asked the reporter.

"One of my guys fell in love with a member of the crew," Benton truthfully replied.

Urlowe remembered the aching sadness on Disson's face when he cradled Korinna's lifeless body. The alien priestess had taken a centaur's arrow for Disson. She was tasked as their guide during the Trials, as an illusion of fairness.

By tradition, she was supposed to die with them anyway. Instead of leading the team into certain death, Korinna listened to her conscience—especially when Disson told her what he loved most about the Earth. Without her guidance, they'd have died within minutes.

Had Benton's men lost the Trials, the Olympians could've claimed the planet. Having tried once before, the aliens were beaten by ancient Greek heroes (whose names were lost to time).

If the aliens won, they'd have harvested the human population for their protein. Korinna explained that it was a key ingredient of T'Ambrosia—a complex drug that allowed the aliens to tap into their innate mystical abilities. Their technology and genetically enhanced slaves were formidable enough. But when Olympians used T'Ambrosia . . .

Well, Urlowe saw enough to understand why the ancient Greeks mistook them for gods.

Korinna told them about the rules, the shortcuts, their pursuers, and how to win. The priestess was swayed by Disson's authentic, "love at first sight" reaction. Because of him, she realized that humans were worth saving.

"When we were offered a chance to see the Olympian Galaxies," lied Benton, "the rest of my team decided to tag along."

The reporter started to ask why but the master sergeant cut her off with a raised hand.

"Before you ask 'why' again, think about it," argued Benton with a mocking grin. "How can you possibly refuse such an offer?! It's like hanging out with Captain Kirk on *The Enterprise*, versus paying bills in this crazy little world of ours. Under different circumstances, I might've gone with 'em."

Murmurs swept through the crowd.

"Is their leader still alive?" asked the reporter.

"He died in his sleep last night," Benton replied with convincing sadness.

Urlowe bit back a grin.

Near the end of the Trials, Disson poured his last mag into Admiral Bikonis' mount. The Olympian fell off his winged pegasus and cracked his skull on a boulder. Before he could regain his senses, Disson pulled his knife and left a dozen holes in that high-and-mighty son of a bitch.

Too bad he couldn't outrun the pack of furies. Disson stood his ground and took them on. Benton and Urlowe (both out of ammo), heard him die as they fled. His sacrifice bought them enough time to guess the Sphinx's new riddle and exit the hunting grounds.

By doing so, Benton and Urlowe denied the Olympians their sizeable harvest—for now. Per the terms of some interstellar code, the invaders couldn't return to this world for another three thousand years.

"So they just left?" frowned the reporter.

"Yeah," nodded the soldier.

"Where to?"

"Home," Benton replied with an evasive smile.

"Where are they from?" she pressed. "And will they come back?"

"Sorry, ma'am. I'm not at liberty to answer either question."

One of the locals pushed his way through the crowd. The skinny, scholarly Greek had olive skin and curly dark hair. Full of zeal, he grabbed the microphone from Benton's hand. Rather than kick the rude man's ass, Benton forced a patient sigh and waited for the obvious question.

"The leader who died—it was Poseidon, wasn't it?" asked the man with a thick accent. "And his two brothers were Zeus and Hades, weren't they?"

Benton hoped his choice of ancient burial sites (on a mountaintop and underground) would make someone reach that incorrect conclusion.

"Sorry friend, I wasn't much into Greek mythology," he replied. "But I did have a *Xena* poster once."

The Greek's look of disappointment was priceless as Benton headed for the passenger door. Military choppers arrived at the scene and began to descend. The crowd reluctantly dispersed as Urlowe revved the engine. Benton slid the cigar back in his mouth and couldn't wait to get his hands on a couple of beers.

The reporter angrily snatched her microphone from the gawking Greek and signaled her cameraman to keep up.

"Is there anything else you could tell us?" she asked with a desperate smile. "Anything at all?"

Benton thoughtfully exhaled smoke as he signaled Urlowe to wait for a second. Then he pulled the cigar from his mouth and gestured for her to come closer.

"Well, ma'am," sighed the master sergeant, "the most challenging thing about the last three days . . . *was your breath*."

With that, he signaled a laughing Urlowe to carry on.

BY THE BALLS

President-elect Desmond Harris paced around the living room of his opulent hotel suite with a triumphant high. At fifty-four, the career politician had a full head of brown hair with gray at the temples. He was also trim, handsome, and charming—assets he carefully used on younger women when his wife wasn't around.

Mounted on a far wall, a large flat-screen showed muted details of his landslide victory. In seventy-six days, the first-term senator from Alaska would be sworn in as the next President of the United States.

There was a knock on the door to his suite.

"Come in," President-elect Harris called out.

Two Secret Service agents were posted just outside. One of them opened the door and let in Ben Pleshel, his campaign manager. The jolly little black man was drunk, fat, and balding. He cradled an expensive bottle of champagne in both hands. On the left lapel of his conservative brown suit was a small mustard stain.

"We did it!" Pleshel triumphantly exclaimed as he danced a little victory jig. "We *diiiid* it!"

Harris' polite smile briefly dimmed as the agent closed the door. That's because the President-elect noticed the evil gleam behind Pleshel's affable eyes. While his campaign manager looked to be in his early sixties, Harris knew better.

"Would you care to do the honors?" Pleshel asked before he handed over the bottle.

Harris graciously popped the cork and looked around for some clean glasses—

When his campaign manager *whipped a pair of them out of thin air.* Unfazed, Harris began to pour.

"Just half for me—*El Presidente*," Pleshel warned. "I'm well past tipsy."

Surprised that demons could even get drunk, Harris set the bottle down and accepted his full glass. The newly elected world leader forced an awkward smile as he tried to think of an appropriate toast.

"To victory!" Pleshel exclaimed with a toothy grin.

Harris politely raised his glass and took a swallow. Pleshel planted himself at the middle of a plush cream sofa. After a quick sip, the campaign manager propped both feet on a coffee table, loosened his red necktie, and noticed the mustard stain. With a frown, he made it disappear, then regarded his "boss" with a cunning smile.

"Now, let's talk about the future," said Pleshel.

"I don't understand," Harris uneasily replied. "I get to call the shots. That was the deal."

"I know," Pleshel conceded. "Now we're *renegotiating* that deal."

"But I signed a contract!" countered the indignant (and nervous) President-elect. "You get my . . . my soul when I die. In exchange, I can run the White House as I see fit. If you want to renege on our deal, then I guess you'll walk away empty-handed."

Pleshel smirked at the human's logic.

"Your argument would be perfectly valid, were it not for one detail: *you're already going to Hell.* That means you'll just end up in some other demon's hands, right?"

Harris' face stubbornly twisted for a moment . . . until he realized that Pleshel had a point. The sum of the politician's many sins would easily qualify him for a place among the damned.

"Also, do keep in mind that I can ruin your presidency with a mere fraction of the dirt I have on you."

To emphasize his point, Pleshel conjured up a woman's high heel and tossed it over to Harris, who instinctively dodged it. The harmless black shoe hit the floor behind him.

"That belonged to the hooker in Juno, the one who overdosed, remember?"

Violently vivid memories of that night crashed through Harris' mind with such force that he staggered back a step.

"That's just the tip of the iceberg," Pleshel warned, before he took another sip.

"What do you want?" Harris asked with a pounding heart.

"A Chief of Staff gig," the demon replied. "Along with a few 'minor' favors along the way."

"How many 'favors'?"

"Three."

"That's all?" President-elect Harris frowned. "I figured you'd be pulling my strings for the next four years."

The demon chuckled in reply.

"Play ball and you'll win your re-election by another landslide," Pleshel vowed. "I'll help you avoid fuck ups, embarrassing moments, and be revered long after you leave office."

"What are the favors?" Harris asked.

"One: the CIA is going to approach you about a black market Russian nuke that's about to get smuggled into the Middle East. Rather than waste time verifying the intel, you'll send in the cavalry and inform the Saudis later."

"I'd have done that anyway," argued Harris.

"No, you wouldn't," scoffed Pleshel. "Your advisors would've cautioned you about the shaky intel and urged you to move through diplomatic channels. You *can't*, because the nuke's gonna wind up in Mecca: during Ramadan. If there's any delay, your response team won't find and defuse the bomb in time."

Harris' face went pale.

Mecca was one of the holiest Islamic cities. During Ramadan, it would be packed with worshippers. Aside from the catastrophic body count, Harris knew to expect all kinds of political and economic chaos, not to mention an escalation in terrorist attacks and regional conflicts.

"Who's behind this?" asked Harris.

The demon hesitated for a moment. "The plot's being hatched by a delusional Russian oligarch. After losing his family in a terror attack, he decided to make all Muslims share in his pain—and rage."

"My people *will* stop this, right?" Harris asked.

"In the nick of time," Pleshel winked. "And once the day is saved, the Saudis will be in our deep and opportunistic debt."

Harris connected the dots quickly enough. "But you're gonna smear the Russians."

Pleshel nodded with a twisted eagerness. "When I'm done, they'll be too busy with random retaliations to mess with our elections or foreign policy."

Harris bit back a chuckle at the hellspawn's sense of national pride. "What about this oligarch?"

"He won't live to see trial," promised the demon.

"I can do that," Harris nodded. "What's the second favor?"

"Well," Pleshel mused, "I've been warned that North Korea will hit South Korea in eighteen months."

"Shit!" chuckled the president-elect. "You're sure about this?"

"Yup," replied the demon. "The North Koreans are moving with the blessing and tactical support of the Chinese. We're talking about years of careful planning, with traitors and saboteurs in key locations. I'd have given them an eighty percent chance of success."

Harris folded his arms for a thoughtful moment. "What's your plan?"

"I'll see to it that Langley gets the verified intel seven months before the invasion," Pleshel assured him.

"What do you need from me?" asked Harris.

"You'll be given a bunch of clever diplomatic options," replied the demon. "Ignore them and discreetly leak it all to the media."

"You don't want me to formally rat them out?" Harris frowned.

"I want you to feign surprise and outrage," Pleshel replied. "The papers will list everything the Chinese and North Koreans did to make this scheme viable. Every bribe, murder, and covert action will be laid bare—in humiliating detail—for the world to see. This shit spans nine other countries, including ours."

"What happens then?" asked the anxious president-elect.

"The international outcry and diplomatic pressures will force China to stand down," replied the demon. "Without their support, North Korea will have to do the same."

"As long as it doesn't turn into a shooting war, I can live with that," sighed Harris, who grew curious about Pleshel's angle. Like the Saudi crisis, all of this hinged on a demon from Hell *not* screwing him over. "And the third favor?"

"During your two terms in office, you're going to have the potential to start five shooting wars."

"Why so many?" Harris asked.

"Diplomacy's not what it used to be," shrugged Pleshel. "But fear not: none of them are major conflicts. Each government could be crushed within a few weeks or less. I need you to commit to each encounter, follow my battle strategies to the letter, then pull your forces out the second you win."

Harris started to object—

"You're not doing any of this 'regime change' crap, Mr. President-elect," Pleshel scowled. "Each country's leadership will remain intact, surrounded by fried infrastructure and angry citizenry."

"Leaving countries to burn isn't exactly our idea of sound foreign policy."

"Neither are insurgencies," Pleshel replied while he admired the manicure on his free hand. "It's cheaper and more effective to just scorch 'em and go home."

A number of Harris' former colleagues on the Hill thought the same way.

"If we're not ending hostile regimes, why make with the 'hit-and-run' warfare?" asked the president-elect.

The demon chuckled at Harris' clever turn of phrase.

"When you flawlessly win five lesser conflicts in a row," explained Pleshel, "we'll be respected and feared again. The American public's willingness to wage war will resurface. And you'll have a much easier time persuading other tyrants to play nice—or risk getting pounded whenever we feel like it."

"I can do that too," said the relieved president-elect, who then finished his glass and poured himself another.

"Good," the demon purred as he rose to leave.

"Mind telling me why you're doing all of this?" Harris asked.

"I thought that would be obvious," frowned the demon.

"Except it isn't," countered the human. "You want to save lives and rein in global tyranny. Why?"

Pleshel emptied his glass.

"Let's just say that God's not the only one who moves in 'strange and mysterious ways.'"

"Huh," shrugged the human. "What about my soul?"

"Do like I say and I'll destroy it when you die," pledged the demon. "No afterlife to worry about. No eternal torment. It's the best type of death for people like you."

Oddly enough, Harris had to agree on that part. "And the new contract?"

"I'll have it in front of you by noon tomorrow," Pleshel replied as he moved across the room. "And this time, don't give me so much grief about signing it in blood, okay?"

"I won't," President-elect Harris earnestly replied. He took a quick swallow from his glass and came up for air when Pleshel reached the door. "One last question."

Pleshel paused, turned, and regarded his partner-in-sin with a look of infernal patience.

"You have me by the balls," admitted the politician. "Why aren't you hell-bent on using this office to wreck America—especially its domestic policies? I mean, there's so much sin to choose from."

Pleshel's face darkened as he dropped his glass and watched it disappear mid-fall.

"Because you humans beat me to that long ago," griped the demon, as he opened the door. "Now, if you'll excuse me, there's a drunken lady staffer who needs my attention."

COPPER FLATS

Shit.

Half the town was ablaze and the stench of death was everywhere. At a glance, I figured we needed more men and some dynamite. We passed an old wooden sign for Copper Flats, Texas. Fresh blood was splattered across it. Whoever died under it got dragged through the dirt, toward the burning heart of this dead town.

I was here with the face and badge of one Ranger Wade Voker. Once upon a time, the cagey lawman thought he was hunting me. Once I fed him to the coyotes and copied his features, I meant to abuse his position for a while then move on. Just as things were getting fun, a frantic telegram came from Copper Flats.

The incomplete message begged for help against something "ungodly."

Normally, I'd ride in the opposite direction. Sadly, Ranger Voker had such a reputation that eight idiots volunteered to help me. Three of them fought for the Confederacy. One was barely old enough to shave. The rest had friends or family in Copper Flats.

Perched atop my black stallion, I found myself with two choices. I could kill my posse and find a new face. Or stupidly succumb to my troublesome curiosity and find out who (or what) killed this damned town. That's why I led them into this freshly minted slaughter.

"Eyes open, guns out, and shoot smart," I called out. "One of the locals might still be breathin'."

Guns drawn, they nervously nodded and followed me in. My guess? They'd blast the first thing that moved wrong. I slid out my Winchester and gripped it with my left hand.

My sisters would've laughed at the sight of me. All stone-faced and ruggedly handsome, with the slicked mustache, fancy clothing, and dual-holstered Peacemakers on my gun belt. None of these sweaty fools noticed my lack of perspiration. If anything, they'd have attributed it to the "Ranger Voker" mystique.

Some of them wore handkerchiefs around their faces, which did little against the stench. The carrion birds had already circled the center of town.

"That way," I ordered.

We rode past burnt-out buildings and several half-devoured horses. They weren't killed by any animal from these parts. No, these mounts were shot dead. Then something heavy crawled over the middle of the carcasses, clawed up their guts, then moved on. Its trail was wider than a stagecoach, with over a dozen overlapping boot tracks on either side.

At the heart of Copper Flats, we found thirty-seven bodies—all women and children. Insects buzzed about, drawn to the free meals. I dismounted with a disgusted frown, bothered by a familiarity with this sort of carnage.

Most of the victims were dressed in their Sunday finest, apparently killed by gunfire, and stacked in a pile. Our youngest member retched at the sight. The rest wanted payback.

Me? I wondered what happened to the menfolk, whose boot tracks led toward the town church— alongside that "ungodly thing." The plain white building resembled an oversized barn with no steeple and a fair need of new paint. While the rest of the buildings were burning or damaged during this massacre, the church was unmarred.

I gripped the reins of my jittery mount and walked toward it. The air got cooler with every step. The source appeared to be the church itself. I signaled the men to surround it. They scattered, collectively eager to get away from the corpses. The flames hadn't reached the saloon (yet), so I tethered my mount to its hitching post.

Some old memory drew me to this slaughter. Perhaps a story I once heard about, before I was banished to this world. Guided by my need to know, I quietly headed for the church's front doors.

By the time I reached the church's entrance, my breath came out as steam. The late Ranger Voker would've been numb in the fingers by now. Born from hardier stock, I didn't slow my pace or show the slightest hint of hesitation. I felt the kid's eyes on me and gave him a reassuring nod. If things went wrong in here, I'd be leaving with his identity.

I quietly opened the left door, slipped in, and closed it behind me.

Inside were the men of Copper Flats. Fifteen, by my count, the dead bastards sat in the front three pews like statues. Where the preacher would have stood was a grayish, kidney-shaped creature. Roughly the size of a stagecoach, it pulsated like a human heart and generated waves of cold as it did so. Icicles and frost covered the windows, walls, and even the corpses.

Shit. A Froku.

The mother sensed my mind and awakened. Fresh out of better options, I aimed at her and emptied the Winchester. White ichor sprayed from the blob's open wounds as the once-living men of Copper Flats awakened too. When the recently deceased turned my way, I could see that their upper torsos were hollowed out.

My grandsires told me tales of Froku and how they killed their victims. Within each chest cavity was a "child" of the mother. Newborn Froku could latch onto a victim with paralytic stingers. They'd eat their way to the spine, bond to it, and grow within the host. By the end of a rapid maturation process, one of them would (likely) outgrow their host body and become a Froku brood mother.

The others would simply become hosts-slash-drones for the new hive: and superior to humans in every possible way. None of these things had matured yet, which was the good news. The bad was that ten of them had iron in their gun belts, which they clumsily drew. The other five simply charged me with a clumsy, communal rage.

A modest aisle separated the church down the middle. Happy to be dealing with amateurs, I dropped the Winchester, whipped out Voker's Colts, and went to work. I ignored the inaccurate return fire and shot the five charging hosts first. Once they were down, I worried about the rest.

Four more of them dropped before a bullet hit my right arm. I glanced down at the green-blooded graze then scowled at my empty Colts. The armed hosts ran out of bullets too, then came at me with bare hands. I holstered my left pistol and went invisible.

Normally, the mother blob could've guided her spawnlings right to me. Guess I filled the bitch with enough holes to distract her. The confused hosts paused and searched me out while I pulled spare shells from my gunbelt.

At the front of the church, the mother Froku shrieked a final cry of anguish, then perished. Hm. Guess I didn't need that dynamite in the first place. Her children turned in unison and erupted into a keening chorus of grief. I used the opportunity to empty my spent shells.

Then I began to walk and reload. One of the gun-toting hosts looked down and spotted my approaching blood trail. Before it could react, I shot the Froku dead from close range. Still invisible (of course), I strolled toward the next one. My boots thunked and my spurs clinked. I was the only one in the room with a ready gun. Each shot had to count, so I needed to get close.

Rather than reload, the remaining five hosts all paused and listened. Two hosts were so close together that I paid them a visit. A pair of shots put them both on the floor. I turned as another Froku rushed in. While it couldn't see me, the creature got lucky and slammed into me mid-turn.

Not in the mood to get stung, I drew my empty Colt with my other arm and stabbed the host with it. A knife would've been better—but I was strong enough to drive the six-shooter's long barrel clean through the Froku blob. That's when the host body became a proper corpse.

Then one of those shit-spawned creatures threw a Bowie knife at me. While I was invisible, it caught my back and missed my fourth heart by inches. I dropped my gun and my concentration. Not only did I turn visible . . . I also slipped into my true form.

Dammit!

Voker was about six feet tall and slim. I was a foot taller and twice his body mass. Every body hair receded under my soot-colored hide. My boots, belts, and clothing all tore apart. The last two hosts regarded me with recognition, then instant hatred. After all, Froku brood mothers passed their memories on to their spawn.

That's how they knew I was an Aikejovian—their most hated foe. My race led the brutal campaign, which destroyed the Froku hive worlds and sent their kind to the brink of extinction. Only a few of the brood mothers escaped.

Fortunately for the human race, I was banished to this remote little world (over a slight political dispute) four decades ago. Had we arrived a few days later, some of the hive spawn would've fully matured. We'd also be facing two (or more) brood mothers and a dozen-plus very agile hosts. Barring a miracle, the Froku would've turned our corpses into new hosts.

Within a decade, they would've had a new hive world to call home.

My three yellow eyes teared up as I ripped the knife free and turned toward its owner. The foul-smelling shit kicker charged in with a wild punch. Before it could land, I stabbed its spawnling with an upward thrust.

That's when the last Froku blob shot out of its host like a wad of tobacco spit. With my chest exposed, it could've stung me with that paralytic venom. I sidestepped the blob and watched it hit the floor with a groan. It started to slide away, until I threw the Bowie knife.

It pinned the damned thing to a wooden floor plank. The last Froku bled a syrupy white ichor, while my body continued to regenerate. I pulled a steel whiskey flask from my torn vest and ignored the blob's agonized shrieks.

The church didn't have windows but it did have doors. So I shifted back into human form, in case any of my posse dared to come "save" me. I wriggled my bare toes, took a healthy swig of whiskey, and pondered my next move.

Froku hives picked up the memories of their hosts—including language skills. All I had to do was make this one talk. Then I'll lead the posse to the ship, kill them, and leave without any witnesses.

With an inspired smile, I emptied the flask's contents onto a relatively dry pew. Then I struck a match and let it fall. Despite the somewhat frozen church interior, the fire caught and began to spread.

"I hope you speak my language," I began with a sadistic grin.

The Froku screamed a shrill response (in fluent Aikejovian).

"Good," I nodded. "Your brood mother must have a ship. Where is it?"

The blob cursed me and my ancestors with an impressive zeal (for such a cute little varmint). I shrugged and nodded toward the growing flames.

"You can waste precious time with the insults," I warned, "or you can tell me what I want to know. Where's the ship?"

The flames fed on the wooden church's interior—and slowly closed in on us both. The only difference was that I could walk right out of here. Bothered by the rising heat, the Froku replied with a series of pitiful squeaks. I folded my arms and gave the creature a most sincere smile.

"Of course I'll let you go," I lied. "You have my word of honor."

DADDY'S HOME

They ran through the night's cold rainfall. The slower guy's name was Aaron. His pal was Vince. Both ex-cons were in their early forties and worked odd crimes to pay the bills.

The streets hardened them and multiple prison stints made them wise. Friends since juvie, they trusted each other more than their own relatives. That bond allowed them to survive and prosper over the years—until last week, when they messed with the wrong little girl.

According to their middleman, some kid saw something she shouldn't have. The client wanted her snatched for a quick twenty thou. Smelling all kinds of risk and heat, they charged double. The client agreed without a fuss.

The job went down two days later.

The brazen crooks did the deed outside of a grocery store, in broad daylight, with witnesses aplenty. Aaron donned a ski mask and grabbed the kid with a chloroform-soaked rag in a gloved hand. Also masked, Vince did the same thing to the girl's screaming grandma. Once granny was down, he covered Aaron with a pair of drawn handguns.

Witnesses ran for cover as Aaron tossed the girl into a pre-stolen station wagon and took the wheel. Vince hopped in the back as his partner hit the gas. Parked six blocks away, in a more secluded lot, was their switch vehicle. Once they moved the girl, they tossed their shirts and masks into the station wagon and torched it.

Within a few short minutes, they casually drove away in a stolen blue minivan. By the time they passed the grocery store, three cop cars were already at the scene. Pleased with themselves, Aaron and Vince delivered the girl to a long-vacant laundromat. The back door was unlocked and their cash was in the basement, as promised. They left the girl in a corner, counted their loot, then left.

That was a week ago.

The kidnapping made the local and national news. They noted the weeping grandmother and requests for viable leads. The newscasters spoke of how poor Kim Lao (their hostage) lost her mom to cancer.

Aaron and Vince figured that the girl was either a corpse or a sex toy by now. After so many victims, they didn't feel much guilt either way. Once their debts were settled, the crooks found themselves with a fair chunk of fun money.

That's why they decided to hit the club that night. Aaron was haggling price with a hot brunette. Vince waited for two beers from the bar.

Then this Asian guy stormed in. Large enough to be a bouncer, he wore drenched street clothes, a low buzz cut, and authentic dog tags. The new arrival seemed to sniff the air . . .

Then he zeroed in on Vince.

The Asian brushed his way through the dance floor without a lick of subtlety. Vince glanced up at the bar mirror, saw trouble headed his way, and turned around. By then, the Asian was on him.

He grabbed Vince by the throat with a firm grip— but not to choke him. Both men were about the same size. Any other time, Vince would've thrown down without a second thought.

Instead, when the big Asian touched him, a deafening chorus of agonized wails erupted *within* the ex-con's mind. The sudden effect left Vince dazed. The hardened criminal fought to drown out the voices and think—or even move. The Asian's dark almond eyes narrowed as he yelled questions about the girl.

Then Aaron stepped up. From three feet away, he put a bullet through the back of the Asian's skull and watched him drop. Vince shook his head as the wailing abruptly ceased.

People screamed, cowered, or ran for the exits. Barely able to stand, Vince let Aaron drag him toward the nearest exit. Out through a side door they ran, along with a few dozen other patrons.

Car horns blew and people clogged the parking lot as they sought to flee. Through the chaos, the pair of career crooks fled on foot. With their records, they needed to get the hell out of town—tonight—before the cops IDed them from the club's security footage.

Behind the parking lot was a microbrewery. The old brick building was closed for the night but had plenty of deep shadows to hide in. They picked one with an awning and ducked under it.

"Who the fuck was that?!" Aaron panted through a smoker's lungs.

"I-I dunno," Vince shakily replied.

"We'll know when they release his name," Aaron replied with an anxious shrug. "Why was he on you?"

"He was askin' about the girl," Vince replied.

"How'd he track us down?" asked Aaron. "That was the cleanest shit we ever did!"

Vince didn't have an answer for that one. Aaron checked his gun and looked around. The rain began to intensify as they stood there.

Vince eyed his watch. It was nine past midnight. "What's the plan?"

Grateful that they carried their extra money, Aaron was about to suggest that they head straight out of state—

"You could always apologize," offered a third voice.

Vince ducked out of his partner's way as Aaron aimed at the voice. Out of the darkened rain stepped the Asian guy. Just as drenched as they were, he looked none too pleased. The rain washed away most of the blood from the back of his head, where the gunshot wound was almost fully healed.

"That's what your friend should do: *apologize*," scowled the Asian. "And, while you're at it, tell me where my little girl is."

"Why ain't you dead, man?!" Aaron half-shrieked. "I put one in your dome!"

"Where is she?!" shouted Kim's irate father.

Aaron rudely shrugged, then cocked the hammer. Vince looked on with tight-lipped apprehension. Neither man would snitch because their client already threw down forty grand to erase a witness. If they talked, that client would likely make them both disappear too. Besides, neither crook knew (or cared) about the girl's fate.

After a few seconds, Kim's father lost patience and pointed at Aaron.

"Take him."

"With pleasure," purred a deep male voice, with a Persian accent, that seemed to come from everywhere.

Aaron started to squeeze the trigger when his gun vanished. The Asian smirked when the weapon reappeared in his right hand. Then an invisible hand plucked Aaron off his feet and dragged him into the rain above.

Vince started to run after his screaming friend, only to stop after a few futile steps. Unable to see through the downpour, both men could hear Aaron's distant shrieks. The kidnapper angrily turned and advanced toward the Asian—

Until Kim's father jammed the handgun against Vince's left eye.

"Give me something useful and I'll let you walk," offered the father. "If you don't, my friend gets you for seconds."

"You're gonna kill me anyway," snapped Vince.

"Maybe," admitted the Asian. "If my girl's hurt or dead? Then you'll die really slow-like. But if my Kimmy's safe, we'll call it even."

The Asian lowered the gun and let his offer sink in. Before Vince could reply, Aaron's corpse landed with a sickening thud upon the asphalt, right in the middle of a handicapped parking spot. Tendrils of steam rose from its slack mouth.

Then a deep, disembodied belch cut through the night. Kim's father smiled at the kidnapper's horrified reaction. "You were saying?"

"Arthur Tinsk," Vince confessed with a defeated sigh. "He's our middleman. If anyone knows who hired us, it's him."

The Asian tossed the gun into the night, turned, and walked off into the dark rain. Surprised to still be alive, Vince was too scared to move. After a minute, the kidnapper heard a sniffing sound. Almost like a massive tiger was right behind him.

"W-what the fuck?!" Vince stammered as he looked around in vain.

"Don't mind me," replied the Asian's invisible partner. "I'm sniffing your soul, just in case I need to find you again."

"You're some kind of demon?" Vince asked.

"I am," he replied. "You could say I followed my 'friend' home from the battlefield. The poor fool thought he had PTSD."

Vince eyed Aaron's corpse and forced himself to think.

"So you possessed him, like in *The Exorcist?*"

"That was the plan," replied the demon.

"I don't get it," Vince frowned. "Why are you helping your victim's kid?"

"That little girl changed everything," explained the demon. "Normally, I'd hollow out his soul and move on to another one—like yours. What saved him was the end of his deployment. Having never been to the 'Land of Opportunity,' I gave him a short reprieve. During that time, I got to know young Kimmy Lao—"

"So? What about her?" Vince interrupted.

An invisible hand seized him by the throat and filled the crook's mind with screams. Vince winced as he recognized one of the wails as Aaron's. The kidnapper dropped to a knee in teeth-grinding agony.

"*I don't know!*" raged the demon with apparent frustration. "What matters is that Kimmy's worth saving."

The invisible, intangible demon flung Vince to the ground and started to leave.

"Whoever has that child will burn inside me for all time," he vowed. "And if she's not perfectly fine when we find her . . . *so will you.*"

DEAD MAN'S TRIGGER

The sudden volley of white plasma fire cut Wordovitz in half. As his armor exploded, the rest of my squad broke for cover. Some of the Death Tree's distant shots punched through the high rubble around me. My Dead Man's AI scanned for probable points of cover and pointed them out with holographic arrows. I picked one, ran like crazy, and dove behind the shattered remnants of a Taco Bell.

Lightning flashed through the radioactive clouds overhead.

"Dolzey! I'm hit!" Scanta bellowed in anguish.

I locked onto her location. Out in the open, she didn't have a prayer.

"Dolzey—!"

A follow-up volley of Death Tree fire silenced Scanta forever. I raised my Omen Rifle and thumbed off the autogun's safety.

"Unit status," I growled.

"You're the only one left," replied my AI's monotone male voice.

Some leader I was. Seven dead in twice as many seconds. I'd give my left nut for a better armor AI. Maybe an artificial intelligence that could express compassion for fallen comrades. Or, better still, a model that could think up brilliant ideas in the face of shitty scenarios (like this one).

"Hostile target entering effective engagement range," the AI announced.

It should've been telling me to run away. Instead, my armor's AI acted as if this op still had a chance.

"No shit!" I snapped. "Remote-launch the Shrouds."

My Dead Man sent the signal as I risked a peek over the rubble. Sensors magnified the image of the floating, tree-like construct. While the Multok surely had a different name for this robotic engine of death, we grunts preferred "Death Tree."

The damned thing looked like a giant, misshapen oak tree (minus the leaves). Made from a super-dense gray alloy, The Death Tree came with a thick trunk and dozens of branch-shaped plasma turrets on top. They came in various sizes and could flexibly bend in almost any damned direction. From top-to-bottom, it was 311 feet high. Its width varied from twenty to eighty feet around.

Worst of all, it could fly.

Roughly a half-mile away, my AI's sensors clocked the Death Tree's progress at a leisurely fifteen miles per hour. Under Shroud cover, my team was supposed to leave a nuke in its path.

The reason for this fool's errand? To give the brass more time to evacuate their field command bunker.

Before the invasion, I expected a nuke to solve most problems. Then the Multok came along and ruined that assumption. On a good day, a Death Tree would fly over a nuke and get vaped in the blast. Then another one would get dropped in within a few hours.

Instead, even with a Shroud strike, the damned things tended to spot the nukes and raise their blast shields before we could get clear. Once their shields were up, our half-kiloton nukes were useless. The blast *might* knock a Death Tree over and do some internal damage (which it could self-repair). Since Wordovitz carried our nuke, all of this was moot.

As the rad rain began to fall, I checked my suit's integrity and external radiation levels—both of which were in the green. I almost felt lucky.

"Shrouds launched and inbound," the AI reported.

Twenty canisters of sensor-jamming nanofog were fired from launchers concealed within Wichita's battle-fucked ruins. I would've preferred twenty nukes but Command wouldn't spare them for one Death Tree. To slow it down, my "Plan B" was to leave all five of my det charges in its path. If its sensors couldn't track 'em in time, the Death Tree might float over them.

Without the shields, a synced blast could damage the exhaust vents and cripple it for a half-hour or so. That would leave Command with enough time to get the hell out of here. From twenty feet high, the war machine was well within the blast radius.

I tensed up as the Shrouds came within visual range. Naturally, the Death Tree's turrets efficiently shot most of the canisters right out of the air. The rest of them got through and harmlessly bounced off its armored hull. The air quickly filled with merging clouds of blue nanofog, which blocked both Multok sensors and minimized standard visibility. The Shroud's camouflage wouldn't last long in this rain.

I rushed out.

The Dead Man armor weighed a half-ton. Thankfully, my AI-enhanced rig didn't slow me down. If I could backflip, it could backflip. Naturally, it augmented my piddly strength a hundred-fold, which allowed me to leap through the fog like an armored bunny with a death wish.

Almost on cue, the Death Tree fired motion-seeking warheads my way. A direct hit would've nailed me with both explosive force and acidic shrapnel. The nanofog made the shots go wide, which counted for something.

I moved through the rain with the grace of an aging athlete. It seemed like an eternity ago that I was teaching gymnastics to little kids in Cleveland Heights. Now, my students were either fighting the war or dead.

Surrender wasn't an option. Rather than bother with prisoners, the Multok executed us on the spot. Hiding from Death Trees was an equally useless idea. Those of us who survived the aliens' weapons died from diseases, fallout, or starvation. If there was a viable place left to hide, I'd have gone AWOL right now.

When the Multok found this world, they ignored our attempts at first contact—then rained some very dirty nukes on us. Why'd they invade? No clue. It wasn't to rule us because they slaughtered most of our population in the first days of the war. Nor was it for any apparent resource, because they indiscriminately torched the world.

Maybe they just wanted a place to park.

Things got so bad that every human survivor was drafted into U.N. Command—starting at age ten. This was a "win-or-die" war with no third option. We were outclassed and losing. In another few years (tops), the human race would be extinct.

Too bad fighting them didn't seem to help much either. The Multok's tech was centuries ahead of ours. Instead of flesh and blood troops, they sent very durable attack drones into harm's way, including Death Trees.

Their people safely lived within massive, bubble-shaped starships. Each one held a massive city, wrapped within a transparent hull. Somehow, the structures moved through space and rained death upon us from stationary orbital positions.

U.N. Command tried to bring them down with everything from fighter bombardments to stealth nukes. None of our weapons could bypass their defensive batteries and force shields. There were nineteen of their ships scattered around the planet—each about the size of Texas.

Well, just because the fight was hopeless didn't mean we were supposed to roll over and die. That's why

I ignored my facial sweat and forced myself onward. The half-mile between the Death Tree and myself turned into a few hundred feet real quick.

Even through the nanofog, I could make out the behemoth's menacing silhouette and its glowing blue exhaust vents. While protocol was to dump the charges and run, I pushed my luck. It was a rare day for anyone to make it this close to a Death Tree. If I could breach through a vent, I'd try to bypass its internal defenses and blow the damned thing from the inside—

A bolt of lightning hit the Death Tree. It struck so quickly that the war machine couldn't erect its shields in time. I skidded to a halt as its thrusters sputtered for a few moments . . . then cut off. The Death Tree simply dropped onto its wide base and went silent.

For a half-second, part of me believed in God again.

"Enemy AI broadcasting distress signal," my AI announced. "Enemy combat firewalls have failed."

It shorted out from a bolt of lightning?! I couldn't believe it.

"Jam its signal!" I laughingly yelled. "Then hack in and eject its AI core."

"Acknowledged," replied the AI.

I found some cover and tensely waited. This was a priceless opportunity. No one had ever captured an intact Death Tree before. Taking its AI would be an even bigger win for us.

The bulk of the human war effort was spent studying the enemy's language, signal traffic, and encryption codes: just for an opportunity like this. With the Death Tree's firewalls down, my AI had the advantage.

We could grab the AI and beeline it for Command. In their hands, we might pull current access codes and God-knew-what-else from it. All I had to do was get it there in one piece.

"Requisition another Shroud launch," I ordered. "Then notify Command on our status."

"The enemy might detect the signal," warned the Dead Man.

"Do it," I gasped. Whether they chose to help or not, Command wouldn't reply (and give away their position). I kept my head down and waited for Act Three to begin . . .

"System infiltration complete," my AI reported, some twelve minutes later. "Death Tree sensors detecting twenty-four inbound Multok Bat Bombers."

I hatefully grinned inside my helmet. Unlike Death Trees, the Bat Bombers were crewed by living, breathing aliens. For them to risk their pilots meant that the Multok were fuckin' scared.

Good.

"Have the Death Tree open fire on them with all weapons," I commanded. "ETA on core eject?"

"Forty-one seconds," the AI replied.

"Good," I muttered, eager to get out of here.

"Assuming command of fire control systems," reported my AI. "Deactivating auto-destruct matrix. Ejection in four seconds."

"Good thinking," I awkwardly frowned. If that thing self-destructed, I'd have been cooked within a multi-kiloton mushroom cloud.

The weapons platform turned all of its branches skyward and opened fire. I held my breath as a small, spheroid object shot out of the center of the Death Tree. No larger than a medicine ball, the alien AI core hovered over to me.

I slung the Omen over my right shoulder and reverently grabbed the white metallic sphere with both hands. Then I turned and ran for dear life. The red, bat-shaped bombers ignored the Death Tree and came straight at me. After some close misses, I realized that I was beyond the nanofog's protective range.

I hoped Command wasn't napping back there . . .

"Inbound Shroud launch detected," replied my AI.

I scrambled behind the ruins of a UPS truck, barely in time to avoid a blast. Another bomber came in to strafe me with its particle guns, only to get picked off by the Death Tree's fire. Its exploding debris harmlessly rained around me and my precious cargo.

Then the next volley of Shrouds came down and filled the area with nanofog. My chances of survival just jumped to two percent. Feeling every bit of my forty-two years, I recklessly sprinted and vaulted for all I was worth. The Dead Man covered tens of yards per leap.

Maybe another unit was inbound to lay down some cover. Otherwise, I'd have to reach one of the rendezvous sites and request extraction. Between the nanofog and the crap thrown around by their bombs, it wasn't impossible.

Then the Bats decided to pattern-bomb the area around me. They dropped everything but last night's garbage. There was no way to dodge it all.

"Warning: likely impact."

I took an impossibly high leap. Something exploded behind me. It was close enough to send me flying. I adjusted my fall, so that the armor ate the brunt of the impact.

As I got up, the integrity alarm went off and indicated acid shrapnel along my rear torso plating.

"Armor integrity failing," warned the AI. "Nine seconds to lethal breach."

I glared up as a Multok Bat swung about for another pass. I was tired enough already. Once the radiation hit me, I'd be done for.

"Assume auto-pilot systems and head for the rendezvous point!" I yelled. "Get this AI to U.N. Command at all costs."

"Order acknowledged," replied the armor, which took over the evasive functions.

Four Bat Bombers popped up on the sensors. Moving in a tight pattern, they got clear of the Death Tree's fire and headed my way. From then on, all I could do was wince as my Dead Man's armor vaulted over debris. While the AI couldn't move as well as I did, we were still in one piece.

Once a full inner breach occurred, I was done for. In this toxic shitscape, I'd have two minutes (maybe), assuming the acid didn't melt through me. The rad nausea began to hit as the Dead Man rushed me through the side of a toppled skyscraper. The Bats streaked away and upward.

My guess? They ran out of missiles and bombs.

Would we make it to the nearest access tunnels? I'd be too dead to care. But it would be worth it if we could figure out a way to kill the Multok with their own tech. The funny thing was how the fate of humanity depended on my AI, which had the personality of a paper bag.

Maybe R&D didn't have to . . . change a thing . . . after all . . .

FOOD

Gloria Cherefield sat under the bright lights of her home's lonely kitchen. The short, skinny blonde was in her late thirties with a despairing beauty about her. Barefoot and full of spite, she wore a faded pair of dirty blue jean shorts and a yellow t-shirt.

Her reddened eyes were fresh out of tears and her last shreds of doubt faded away—hence the loaded gun in her lap. Life had fallen to such abysmal lows that a bullet to the brain was better than facing tomorrow. Suicide was the only way Gloria could erase the shame of losing the family farm.

The bank denied her another extension. She wasn't surprised, seeing as they were eager to foreclose and sell the land. And it all happened on her watch.

Pa's prostate cancer treatments annihilated their savings and forced them into debt. Then her fiancée ran off with some stripper he was banging on the sly. For once, the crops were good and the markets were better. Gloria just couldn't keep up with the bills and labor demands. Her pa would've found a way to pull through. Now he was gone.

The proud woman even asked for help from the rest of the family. While they were all sympathetic, none of them stepped up in a meaningful way. To save the farm, what Gloria needed was cash, manpower, or a brilliant way to delay the inevitable. The best her useless relatives could do was to stack her kitchen table with food. That was two days ago, after the funeral, when the idea of suicide took root.

Now, without further ado, she picked up the dull gray .44 Magnum. Her pa bought it in the '70s (after watching a bunch of *Dirty Harry* movies). Gloria checked the revolver again, even though she knew it was loaded.

Then she considered a suicide note and pulled a notepad off the top of the fridge: the same one she used to make Pa's funeral arrangements. A blue pen was still clipped to it. With a hateful sigh, Gloria put her gun down and worked on a scathing note. Halfway through it, there was a heavy pounding on the door.

She glanced up at the old clock over the fireplace. It was almost midnight on a Monday. Gloria curiously walked through the living room, toward the insistent pounding.

A month ago, she would've answered the door with the .44 and a healthy bit of caution. Her current sense of despair negated any concerns about who'd be on her porch this late at night. Not in the mood for visitors, Gloria opened the door—

"*FOOD!*" shouted a dozen undead abominations as they stumbled inside.

Gloria screamed and ran for the kitchen, certain that a zombie apocalypse had started without her. Each of them wore rotted, double-breasted suits. Covered in dirt, their flesh regenerated by the second. Too frightened to notice that detail, Gloria grabbed the Magnum, put her back to the kitchen sink, and aimed for the nearest undead.

What stayed her trigger finger was a hard fact. Twelve zombies and six bullets didn't leave her with good odds.

"Get away from me!" she shouted. "I-I have a gun!"

The mass of walking dead ignored her as they scattered about the kitchen. Two of them smashed into the cookie jar and fed on *Fig Newtons* with a semi-feral greed. One of them threw open the kitchen cabinet and ripped open vegetable cans like they were made of cardboard. The rest of them went for the food in the fridge, which they stacked on the table.

Gloria inched around a pair of feeding zombies and made her way to the back door. On the other side of it was the backyard. Only when she reached it did Gloria look back and notice the advanced rate of their regeneration.

The sight of it left her speechless.

In just under a minute, they were licking the crumbs off her table *and looked very much alive*. When the smelly intruders finally noticed her, Gloria put the gun to her head.

"You ain't turnin' me into no damned zombie!" she shouted.

"'Zombie'?" one of them asked with a thick Chicago accent. The others moved behind him, like he was in charge. "What's a zombie, toots?"

Gloria paused for a moment.

"You know! The *undead*!" she argued. "They come back to life and eat people! That means you're all zombies . . . right?"

They glanced over at each other for a moment, then enjoyed a group laugh at her expense—until one of them checked his pulse.

"Shit!" he exclaimed. "We *are* dead!"

The other zombies still didn't believe it, until they checked their vitals. Gloria frowned at their varied reactions, which ranged from confused to scared. A few even crossed themselves.

"Lady, I don't know what happened to us," said the lead zombie. "As long as we're on this side of the grass, I could care less."

"How'd you die?" Gloria asked.

The zombies paused for a moment. Then scowls crossed their faces.

"We were moving a few trucks of whiskey," replied the leader. "Along the way, we got ambushed."

"Who killed you?" she asked.

"Doesn't matter now," shrugged the lead bootlegger. "Next thing I know, we woke up under some fancy road, dug ourselves out, and found all these glowing pink rocks nearby—"

"Meteors," one of the other bootleggers interrupted. "They're called 'meteors.'"

Gloria remembered reading about last week's meteor shower, which happened not too far from the farm. Their tiny town paper devoted a few paragraphs to the stellar event.

"Whatever," the leader replied. "At first, we looked like shit. Then we started healing up real fast. It left us hungry as hell. Soon as we could move, we went looking for food. The first place we found was yours."

With clear embarrassment, the lead bootlegger paused to take in the messy kitchen.

"And now," he winced, "we've eaten you out of house and home. Sorry about that."

"So you're not gonna eat me?" Gloria asked.

"We've been rude enough for one night," chuckled the undead bootlegger.

Gloria sighed with relief and lowered her gun. One of the other zombies picked up her half-finished suicide note and gave it a read.

"Hey boss," the zombie frowned as he held up the paper. "This dame was gonna ice herself."

The leader sized up Gloria's work-hardened frame and felt a bit horny in his regenerated loins.

"Now why would you wanna end your life?" he asked.

"I'm about to lose my farm to the bank tomorrow," Gloria replied, as her sadness returned like a sudden weight.

"Are you now?" scowled the lead bootlegger. Having lived (and died) during the Great Depression, he didn't care much for bankers—neither did his crew.

"Boys!" barked the leader, "I think we owe this lady a favor. Some banker's gonna put her in the poor house. Maybe we should have a 'chat' with him."

The reanimated zombies' malicious grins made Gloria take a nervous step backward . . .

*　*　*

A year later, her farm was halfway out of the red. The markets weren't as good as last year's, but the harvest yield was above par. The president of the local bank was "persuaded" to grant Gloria one final extension. A late-night visit, from twelve angry zombies, might've had something to do with that decision.

Gloria half-expected her odd saviors to leave soon after. Only, after eighty-seven years in the ground, the bootleggers were light on money or options. In return for free room and board, they offered to stick around and work the farm (until they could figure out their next moves).

Once she taught them the basics, the ex-mobsters stepped up. To Gloria's amazement, they handled the fields, animals, and upkeep without a word of complaint. They only needed a few hours' sleep per day and were pretty damned strong. When the tractor broke down, two of the zombies unhitched the plow and pushed the tractor across the field and into the barn!

They spent most of their free time on her computer or at the town library. While they all ate like crazy, they did live on a farm. Also, a few of her lonely cousins were more than happy to help with the cooking. At first, even with the extra help, Gloria wasn't sure they could turn a profit in time. But the leader of the bootleggers—Anthony Vitoglia—assured her that all would be made right. Then, every so often, a few of Anthony's guys would leave the farm for a few days.

After they came back, Gloria would read something about an armored truck getting knocked off the road by masked hijackers with superhuman strength. The police never came knocking at her door because every heist was done in a different state. Clearly, they read up on the tricks of modern-day crime and forensic science.

Once she was back on her feet, Gloria expected Anthony's crew to leave and become full-time crooks again. While they offered her a piece of their ill-gotten loot, Gloria was too honest to take a penny and too grateful to judge them. When (or if) their actions caught up with them, she meant to have their backs in any (legal) way she could.

As far as Gloria was concerned, these undead gangsters were family—just of a different sort.

GUNZ, PAPER, SCISSORS

Just before my murder, Candace told me about this little-known Midtown detective agency with a silly name. The local paper mentioned them after they solved a number of peculiar homicides over the last year; cases that stumped both the police and the FBI. While I forgot the details or even the name of the firm, I fantasized about them taking my case and succeeding where the police failed.

Then again, I was too dead to ask anyone for help.

Three months ago, I was a family man with a mortgage and a pulse. Then someone shot me from behind, while I was dropping off my dry cleaning. I remember an abrupt pain, falling down, dying, and the strain of not crossing over. It was like being the rope in a tug-of-war between this world and the hereafter.

By the time my ghostly form manifested, my killer was long gone. It was strange to stare at my lifeless corpse and watch people gawk down at me like roadkill. Whoever did this left me to die and didn't steal a thing.

The police showed up and investigated the scene with due diligence. I watched them try for a few weeks, hoping that they were smart or lucky enough to solve the case. Sadly, they weren't.

I should have been in the afterlife, earning whatever eternity had to grant me. Instead, I was a restless spirit in search of justice. I should've let it happen . . . but none of it made sense!

I hadn't been in a fight since I was twelve. I was just a regular guy. My worst enemy was old Mrs. Finkley who lived next door. The crone loved to call the cops whenever I played the drums in my garage.

I couldn't think of anyone who wanted me "dead" dead. I had to know who killed me and why. Those questions haunted me harder than I could ever haunt this world.

Not knowing why you are a ghost was almost as annoying as actually being one. I didn't glow, float around, or have transparent features. My condition cloaked me from all five senses. Animals couldn't spot me. I couldn't even see my reflection. Unlike a proper poltergeist, I couldn't possess people or do anything cinematically cool. With enough concentration, I could become solid for a minute or two. My other useless "super powers" were intangibility, permanent insomnia, and no need for food or drink.

Worst of all was the loneliness.

Being a social person in life, I was talking to myself more and more in death. Since my murder, I hadn't found one other ghost. With the large number of violent deaths in this world, that just didn't make sense. There should be more of us running around with unfinished business.

Of course, there might be ghosts all over this damned city and we just couldn't see each other. Then again, another ghost could be indistinguishable from a living person. I think I'd have to see one do something "ghostly" to even know the difference.

Tortured by this situation, I strolled through Midtown. It was a bright autumn afternoon. I was busy moping about when this honey-hued fox of a woman walked past me. In her early forties, she looked exotically Middle Eastern, with a revealing white blouse, black purse, and gray slacks.

In her brown designer boots, she was a bit taller than me. Her hair was lengthy and black. Some kind of bug-shaped metal amulet hung snugly above her naturally impressive cleavage.

While I admired her a few seconds too long, I figured that it was okay to gawk, being dead and all. But instead of passing me by, she stopped and gently took me by the arm.

"Pardon me, but how long have you been dead?" she asked with a slight accent that I couldn't quite place.

I was too shocked to answer at first.

"T-three months," I managed. "Are you another ghost?"

"No. I'm a sorceress," she replied with an understanding smile and an offered right hand. "Amelia Dushoy."

"Ed Tannsley," I replied with a vigorous handshake.

She gave me a knowing smile, then pulled her hand away.

"Um, sorry," I said.

"Why are you still on the mortal coil?" she asked.

"Somebody killed me," I blurted out with erupting hope. This was awesome! Amelia might know some way to find my killer.

"I-I need to know who did it. *Please*, can you help me?" I begged.

Amelia opened her purse and pulled out a large, roughly hewn white stone. Triangular in shape, it reminded me of a prism, only it was milky-white inside.

"Murdered, huh?" Amelia sighed with a hint of pity. "That's terrible."

"What's with the stone?" I asked.

"Well," Amelia casually explained, "I don't run into free-walking ghosts very often. When I do, I like to capture their souls and use them to enhance my magic or sell them on the black market."

I let her words and facial expression sink in for a moment.

"You're evil, aren't you?"

Amelia shrugged and nodded as she moved to tap me with the white stone. Well, I felt bad that I couldn't get any help or even post-mortem nookie out of this attractive woman. Oddly enough, that last thought went through my mind as I went solid and kicked her between the legs.

The sorceress dropped the stone and fell to her knees with a wail of pain. As luck would have it, three street punks were tailing Amelia before she found me. Thinking her a juicy target, they rushed her doubled-up form and whisked her into a narrow alley.

One snatched her purse while the other two argued over who'd do her first. I turned and ran for my existence because something told me that Amelia wasn't that kind of victim. A few seconds later, a powerful explosion roared out of the alley. Even intangible, I felt the shockwave.

Had I not been a block away, I might've gone flying. One of the punks, minus his legs, soared over me then crashed (headfirst) through the side window of a parked Jeep Wrangler.

I stopped at the jeep, made a sharp right, and fled through a half-dozen terrified witnesses. I ran through a row of buildings, up flights of stairs, and into a fifth-floor hallway. Pleased not to be sweaty and winded, I paused to get my bearings. At the end of the long hallway was a door with a familiar but silly title:

Gunz, Paper, Scissors
Private Investigators

These were the guys I read about, before I died—
"TANNSLEY!" Amelia's voice echoed through the halls, like she was in the building. How'd she find me? Oh. Right. She was a sorceress.

I headed for the detective agency. I planned to jump through the door and try to lose her somehow. If she followed, then Amelia might be delayed by these private eyes. It was a selfish, cowardly thought but I was out of choices.

Instead of passing through the wood-and-glass door, I bounced off so hard that I landed on my ass. While the glass didn't even crack, my face hurt! The door opened and out stepped a lanky guy in his mid-forties.

His slicked-back hair and eyebrows were unnaturally white. The guy was nerdy-looking but not in a benign way. More like a white-collar criminal or a dental interrogator. Dressed in a gray three-piece suit, he pushed up a pair of wire-rimmed bifocals.

"May I help you?" he asked.

I scrambled to my feet. "You can see me too?!"

"That I can—" the man started to say, before he tackled me. We both hit the floor as a bolt of crackling white energy raced over us, into the office, and through the female receptionist inside. The upper half of her plump, middle-aged corpse slammed into the coffee machine and hit the floor with a shocked look on her face.

I looked up as Amelia strode toward us from the opposite end of the hallway. Covered with dirt and someone else's blood, she approached in a red-faced rage. As I stood up (again), the white-haired man winced at his dead receptionist.

"Damn!" he grunted. "Third temp this year!"

Office doors up and down the hallway opened as folks ran past her for the nearest exit. Someone pulled a fire alarm on the way out. Amelia spotted me and started to smile, until the white-haired man jumped to his feet. With a scowl, he turned her way and drew a drum-fed machine gun from his tiny vest pocket!

Even Amelia backed up a surprised step and quickly yelled something as he opened up at full-auto. I thought he was quick enough. Then a bluish dome formed around her in the last possible instant.

He fired with a two-handed grip and didn't miss once. There should've been shell casings all over the place (except there weren't). That cannon also should've run out of bullets by now . . .

Oh. He was a mystic too. Well, even with a magic gun, his slugs splattered against her barrier with no apparent effect.

A boy's voice with a hillbilly accent yelled something I couldn't hear. I turned around to see a little kid in a beige cotton suit. Maybe ten or eleven, he wore some kind of coppery utility belt around his waist. On each wrist was a rectangular metal bracer.

"What the hell's goin' on, Gunz?" shouted the boy, just as Gunz paused his barrage.

"Possible client," he replied with a nod my way. Then he resumed firing.

While Amelia's dome held, her face clearly showed signs of strain. If Gunz kept firing, he might've cracked it. The sorceress must've thought so, too. Maybe that's why Amelia ripped the amulet off her neck and tossed it beyond her mystical dome.

The instant it hit the floor, the amulet quickly sprouted legs and began to grow. Made of metal, the eight-legged monstrosity hungrily scuttled into Gunz's gunfire. Damned thing stopped growing at about six feet high and took up the width of the hallway.

Worst of all, his weapon didn't even scratch its surface.

"Go wake up Paper!" the kid yelled as he crossed his arms. "We wouldn't want her to sleep through this!"

Gunz gave a grim nod as the kid's bracer-thingies sprouted serrated blades—kind of like swords. He dashed for the monster while Gunz headed back into the office. I figured the kid to be crazy and would've told him to get out of here: *if he wasn't so damned fast.*

The boy ran sideways along the right wall, dodged the thing's pincers, then sank both blades through its head. The abomination squealed, slumped onto its belly, then disappeared. He nimbly landed and spotted the amulet.

"Don't know who you are, lady," warned the kid, "but you wanna vanish before my granny gets here."

"Out of my way, brat!" Amelia yelled as she waved her hand.

An invisible force lifted the kid off his feet and slammed him into a concrete wall—just to the left of the office door. Instead of ending up a bloody smear, the "boy" left a deep dent in the wall. As plaster fell, he retracted his wrist blades and tapped his belt buckle.

"Have it your way," the kid scowled.

Red-and-gray armor seemed to pour out through his suit. Vaguely medieval in style, it covered him from boots to visored helm. There was an emblem on the upper-left chestplate and the middle of his back—both of a large pair of gray scissors.

Somehow, a child-sized katana appeared on his left hip in a red scabbard. The kid rolled to his feet, deftly drew his blade, and wielded it in a two-handed high guard.

"Scissors!" Amelia gasped with recognition. "If you're here, then—"

I felt (rather than heard) a new arrival behind me. Somewhat afraid, I turned around. In the doorway of the office stood a gray-haired woman. She looked about seventy and wore a blue-and-white flower print dress that clashed with her orange Crocs. Thick red glasses covered her thin, wrinkled, and cranky face.

Were it not for the ball of fire in her right hand, she would've reminded me of Mrs. Finkley. Then I glanced at the office door, as Gunz ran up behind her with his huge hand cannon at the ready.

"Amelia Dushoy," Paper nodded as the flames illuminated her smoke-stained grin. "You would be stupid enough to ruin my afternoon siesta."

The sorceress desperately eyed her amulet and yelled out something in a garbled language. Three dozen armored 'things' appeared around it. While they were humanoid, their scaly blue skin and single-eyed faces were anything but. Their armors were all black-and-yellow and they carried wicked-looking fighting spears.

With an inhuman roar, they charged us. Gunz opened fire with eerie precision. His bullets knocked them down but little else. Scissors waded into them like he was some samurai/Zorro hybrid. Yellowish blood and body parts were flying . . . until the fight was over.

Paper stifled a yawn and gave me an "I-got-this" sneer.

Amelia tried to run. Paper uttered something guttural, and the sorceress disappeared with a surprised yelp. An instant later, I heard her screams: from inside the ball of mystical fire!

Paper held it closer, so that I could see into it. Despite the heat, I approached and saw a miniaturized Amelia Dushoy. Chained to a pillar of stone, flames consumed her. Instead of disgust, I felt a guilty pleasure at watching the evil bitch burn to death. Seconds later, there was nothing left but the pillar and chains.

Paper dispersed the ball of fire and surveyed the slaughter. Gunz tucked the machine gun back into his vest. As he did, all of his bullet holes disappeared from view. Scissors pulled his blade out of the last dead conjuration. Then he stabbed his sword through the amulet and split it in half. Once he did that, the bodies vanished—gore and all. The hallway almost looked perfectly normal.

Paper snapped her fingers and turned my way as the fire alarm went silent.

"So you've come here for help?" asked the old woman.

"Um . . . yeah," I cowered. "Not just from that crazy sorceress lady. Someone killed me and I'd like to know who and why."

Paper carefully examined me.

"How long have you been dead?"

"About three months."

"Then you don't have any money to pay us," Paper replied with an impatient sigh.

She turned back toward the office, probably to resume her nap. I started to leave, oddly grateful that Paper didn't cook me too. Gunz cleared his throat and regarded the charred remains of their receptionist.

The old lady eyed the corpse, then her grandson, whose armor poured back into his clothing. The kid adjusted his lapels and glanced me over.

"C'mon, Grandma!" Scissors pleaded. "His aura's cleaner than a puppy's. Let's help him."

Paper folded her wrinkled arms and silently weighed my fate for a moment.

"How fast do you type?" she asked.

IGNORED

In need of a stiff drink, Zoe started to wonder if she was losing her damned mind. To her relief, a uniformed server wove around guests and approached with a tray of champagne glasses. Zoe tried to flag her down, only to get ignored. Undaunted, she waited for another one to pass by.

When the next approaching server also seemed to pay her no mind, Zoe rudely snatched two glasses from his tray. Some champagne splashed across the right side of his face. She winced as it rolled down the server's white uniform shirt collar and black bowtie.

"Oh! I'm so sorry!" Zoe called out.

Without any kind of reaction, the server kept going (wet face and all). The assistant-slash-aspiring-actress downed one glass and carefully set it on a low table in Julian Trost's opulent living room. The furnishings alone were worth more than a year of her acting school tuition.

Forced to drop out (for now), she found a job in Trost Production's L.A. branch. Last week, in a rare display of generosity, Zoe's demanding boss personally invited her to this party. After six months of long hours and crap pay, she never expected Julian to do such a thing.

Trost's weekend place was in the mountains and took her almost three hours to reach.

The villa was semi-packed with two types of guests. There were the "beautiful leeches," who schmoozed and enjoyed fancy hors d'oeuvres while they sought opportunities. Then there were those they gravitated around. These were the industry elites: the ones who could easily make or break careers. Money dripped off everything they wore, said, and did—no matter how trivial.

While Zoe was from Minnesota, she had spent enough time in New York and L.A. to distinguish between both groups. She could tell that most of this evening's guests were pretenders. In all likelihood, they spent themselves into debt to look the part.

Then again, she was a pretender herself.

An invite to this party implicitly demanded top-notch attire that Zoe didn't have. Living hand-to-mouth since high school, all of her outfits were suitable for bar trips and church. With her credit cards all but maxed out, Zoe hit a secondhand store and got lucky.

Some idiot parted with an older Blave St. Krimm party dress. While filmmaking was Zoe's passion, she knew her way around fashion too. At first glance, she thought it to be a damned-good knockoff, until her fingers touched that black and red silk. While it wasn't as good as a Versace, the outfit was perfect for this occasion.

Better still, the dress was just her size. She walked straight out of the fitting room, dropped thirty bucks, and went home to accessorize her new find. During the ride over, Zoe had plenty of time to think up some kind of strategy.

In the end, she decided to go in "soft," which meant listening more than talking. Perhaps a friendly approach would make a good impression on someone worth knowing. It was the longest of long shots, for a dream which dimmed by the birthday.

More than anything, Zoe wanted to be an A-list actress and star in some iconic films. That wasn't the only part of her dream. Once she established herself in film, Zoe wanted to get behind the scenes, where the real power was. She currently had ten solid screenplays, all proofed and ready to pitch.

By the time someone wrote her obituary, Zoe wanted it to include how she became a director and opened her own production business. The long odds didn't scare Zoe one damned bit. No, giving up the dream (after sacrificing so much) was her truest nightmare.

One hour into the party and her soft strategy failed miserably. Anyone Zoe approached ignored her, from absolute strangers to some of her friends from work. Even the staff didn't acknowledge her—and it was their job to be nice to everyone.

Zoe downed the second glass as Julian Trost entered the room. His slight frame masked heavyweight influence. The nephew of Brolan Parks (her favorite director), Julian started at the middle of the ladder but earned his spurs.

These days, her boss made hit films on four continents. While the production budgets were so-so, the results weren't. Trost's office was lined with two dozen lesser film awards and press clippings of sixteen Oscar nominations—each rightfully earned. With his resources and talent, it was only a matter of time before he brought one home.

Trost was tough but kind. Sympathetic but distant. When he invited her here, Zoe figured it was a discreet compliment laced with opportunity. She wouldn't waste it.

The lovely assistant checked herself out in a platinum-lined wall mirror, then waited for Julian to make the rounds. Her boss chatted up a few of his guests. When he started to leave the room, Zoe made her move.

"Julian!" she sincerely gushed, "You have a beautiful home."

He walked past Zoe without even a glance. The assistant wondered what the hell was going on. She walked over to a handsome, light-skinned guest with a mop of tiny braids in his hair and overpriced clothing.

Just to be a bitch, she repeatedly poked him in the nuts with her right index finger. Her eyes widened when the man didn't react one bit. Dread trickled through Zoe as she snatched the mostly empty martini from his hand and downed it. He ignored the theft of his glass and (without missing a beat) continued his flirty conversation with a busty blonde.

"Am I dead?" Zoe whispered to herself. "I've gotta be a ghost or something. Nothing else makes sense—"

"You're not a ghost," replied a husky, female voice.

The startled assistant looked down, then froze where she stood . . .

"I can also promise that you're not dreaming, crazy, or in the middle of a hidden camera prank show," added Zoe's used dress. The dress was *talking* to her?!

"Someone spiked my drink," Zoe said to herself. "Yeah, that follows. I must be high right now."

"Nope," replied the Blave St. Krimm. "I'd have warned you."

Zoe whimsically wondered if anyone would even notice this bizarre conversation. After all, they ignored everything else she did.

"So, you're a talking Blave St. Krimm dress?" Zoe asked with a shaky smile.

"Pretty much," it confirmed.

"But how?" Zoe pressed.

"It's complicated," the dress eventually replied. "Let's just say that everyone's ignoring you because I'm telling them to, in a 'subliminal' sort of way."

Zoe frowned as she took in the other guests. "You can do that?"

"Uh-huh," replied the dress. "Whatever I say, they'll do."

"How'd you end up in a thrift shop?" Zoe asked.

"That's another long, messed-up story," the dress evasively replied. "Now, what are *you* doing here?"

"Trying to get into the acting game," she confessed.

"That's too bad," sighed the Blave St. Krimm. "You're in a meat market orgy that'll start once they realize you're here."

"Why?" asked Zoe.

"Because you're the guest of honor," replied the dress. "That's why your boss really invited you."

"But Julian's married," Zoe countered, suddenly aware of the intimate interactions around her.

"Like that's an issue," scoffed the dress. "As long as it stays out of the press, their marriage is wide open. She gets her kicks and Julian gets his."

"How do you know that?" Zoe doubtfully asked.

"I've heard a lot of little tidbits that your ears haven't picked up," it explained. "For example, Julian wants to show you his 'sweat cave'. It's downstairs, comes with assorted bondage gear, and has a pair of assless Chaps in your size."

"That's crazy! I'd never have sex with my boss," Zoe fumed.

"Heh! That's what the last three assistants said, according to the gossip," replied the dress. "Your male colleagues are looking forward to the sex tape."

Zoe folded her arms and resisted the urge to take another drink. Maybe this talking dress was full of shit. Or Julian really meant to bend her over in his private bondage room . . .

"I should go," she sighed.

"You could do that," said the dress. "Or I could wrap Julian around your finger and give you a wicked leg up in this business."

Zoe paused for a moment. Stubbornly convinced that this was some cruel joke, she kicked off her shoes. Then she did twenty jumping jacks—near the center of the room—and rotated (clockwise) as she did so. Zoe expected someone to break character and react. No one paid her a single hint of attention.

"Pretty cool, huh?" asked the dress as Zoe leaned against a wall and put her heels back on. "They think you're running late."

"Why haven't you hypnotized me?" she asked, breathing hard and feeling the fool.

"Anyone who wears me is immune," replied the Blave St. Krimm. "I also have a basic obligation to get you whatever you want. So, if you want to become an actress, say the word and I can have you signed to a decent flick in a matter of weeks."

"What's the catch?" the assistant asked.

The dress went silent for a while.

"I want to be hand-washed on a weekly basis," it replied. "And there are some shows and movies I want to catch up on. And, of course, you have to maintain this dress size."

All but certain that there was a higher price to pay down the line, the aspiring actress could've refused. Instead, she saw an opportunity and took it.

"You've got a deal—as long as you can deliver," Zoe promised.

That's when the surrounding chatter abruptly stopped and everyone in the living room dropped to both knees. With all eyes squarely on Zoe, they reverently bowed until their heads touched Julian Trost's expensive carpet.

"That won't be a problem, Zoe," vowed the dress. "Not at all."

KNIGHT OF THE MOTORCYCLE

My double-edged luck never ceased to amaze me.
I was kicking back in a Myther's Ridge bar, with a brew in my hand and a busty waitress in my sights. There were silver pieces in my pocket and I meant to spend them on a decent drunk-on. What was the occasion? I had to celebrate another successful (albeit messy) heist that my crew pulled off just last week.

My twenty bikers went up against ten Treasury guards and a currency train's very accurate side cannons. The original plan was to ride up on our cycles and board it, under the cover of darkness. Barring an unlucky guard, I meant to do this job without a shot fired. My crew were all sneaky bastards, seasoned 'jackers, and more than capable.

Before we could board the train, someone spotted us. Heavy machine guns slid out and we scattered like cats in a dog pound. As my guys died around me, I radioed ahead to Carter—our demo expert. If we couldn't take the train with finesse, he'd blow the rails.

The charges were placed well ahead and made a wicked bang. Unable to stop in time, the train derailed. Out in the Neo-Arizona Desert, we had a good hour before the nearest backup hoped to arrive.

When we regrouped, Carter included, only five of us were still breathing. They were thrilled with the idea of bigger shares and future spending sprees. I knew better.

After a mess this big, there'd be a lotta heat. Traceability was always my biggest worry. After all, the easier you were to track, the sooner the bounty killers came gunning for you. That meant I had to cancel the next two scores, scatter these guys, and put together an entirely new crew.

We gunned down a few wounded guards and blew open the train's six onboard vaults with acid charges. Naturally, we ignored the paper money. Outside of the remaining city-states (and their stiff surveillance grids), Ben Franklins no longer mattered.

That's why we went for the precious metals. I wasn't a fan of gold—either as coins or irregularly shaped nuggets. Like cash, the shit could be tracked with the right tech.

Rare earth metals were often tagged and a bitch to cleanly fence—even if I took the time to melt it down. Besides, any biker who spent gold with reckless abandon typically ended up swinging from a lawman's noose or shot in the back.

I liked silver because it raised fewer questions. Also, the Treasury didn't bother laser-coding nuggets (yet). A friend once told me this loophole was intentionally preserved within the city-states, to allow for all kinds of back-alley bribes and skimming.

My guys scoffed at the silver because it wasn't worth as much. Fully aware of the risks of tagged metals, they loaded up on them anyway. Shit, why not? With four times their expected shares, they babbled on about sweet retirement. They said their farewells and rode for the Mexican border tunnels.

As I loaded up on silver nuggets, I expected them all to end up dead or in a Mexican jail by month's end. I also assumed one or more of them would give me up. That's why I fed 'em a crock of shit about lying low in the Seattle Woodlands, with some post-hippie chick named Yolanda.

Then I made for the Utah Badlands.

As I watched the remnants of my old gang roll off, I thought back to my dad. He taught me how to read, shoot, ride a cycle, and (by default) what not to do when 'jacking trains for a living.

Dad was a smart man with a serious rep. Too bad he loved being the notorious outlaw. He had a small gang of 'jackers under his thumb. Called "Knights of the Motorcycle," the nomadic crew managed to last six whole years before ending up dead in '59. Ma refused to let me join. So I waited for the lung cancer to finish her off, then went through their challenging initiation process.

A week before I would've earned my colors, Dad got busted taking on a passenger train. He tried to blend in but someone recognized him from the wanted posters. Things went sour after that. Three of his guys were killed by security agents. He and the rest were rounded up, given a speedy trial, then hung a few days later.

As I watched Dad swing from a noose, I decided to become a student of crime. Unlike my brothers of the chrome, I couldn't afford to be a one-dimensional thug. I had to pay attention to the world—both in terms of how it currently worked and how it used to. Knowing that distinction has saved my ass more than once.

That's why I took the back roads until I rolled into Utah. Just over the territorial border was Myther's Ridge: the best source of cold beer for a hundred miles. It was also an oasis of outlaws, pussy, and contraband.

Granted, lawmen and bounty hunters would be on our trail. But here's the thing: all the witnesses on that train were dead. We shredded its interior surveillance grid before we left. Being long-haired and bearded, Myther's Ridge was a far better place to hide than Mexico (even though my Spanish was up to par).

To top it off, I went by multiple aliases—even when dealing with trusted 'jackers. A versatile identity was vital at beating the gruesome odds of my chosen profession. The second my real name appeared on a wanted poster, I'd retire: on the grounds of terminal stupidity.

This sprawl of cheap buildings was built around an old football stadium. After significant mods, it became an honest-to-God brewery. Their Ridge House beer was a regional favorite. Around the facility were farms, bars, brothels, and other businesses which relied upon the beer-making juggernaut.

While I'd been through here dozens of times, I kept to myself and didn't earn a rep of any kind. I was just another sweaty face in the crowd. A few of the whores might've remembered me by the bullshit aliases I'd used in the past (from Bob Marley to Dick Cheney). For this trip, I decided to go by "Dean Martin."

I'd crash here for a few weeks. During that time, I'd quietly convert my silver to cryptocreds. I might even get some facial alteration surgery.

Then I'd roll for the Vegas Crack. One of the few cities to get leveled during the Sterility War, "Sin City" had the rotten luck of being saturation-bombed during an 8.4 earthquake. It simply amazed me that anyone lived, much less decided to rebuild around a giant crack in Mother Earth's ass.

The casinos and brothels weren't bad but Dad hated the place. He used to swear that it was a "shadow of its former glory."

So there I was, sipping a Myther's Ridge beer and thinking of Vegas, when the brewery's external alarms went off. Huge and loud, the damned sirens could be heard from miles away and cut through the bar's music and chatter.

The sirens only blared in the face of an external attack, which hadn't happened in almost twenty years. I wonder who'd be crazy enough to hit a town with over a thousand armed bikers running around. We may be rabble but we're mean, dangerous rabble.

Also, Myther's Ridge didn't survive this long without its own security force. On a normal day, they'd stay out of the town and leave us to settle our disputes in an "eye-for-an-eye" kind of way. Security only swooped in to break up the occasional riot or settle a brewery-related matter.

Well-armed and better-trained, they could've come out here and fought alongside us bikers. I knew they wouldn't because Myther's Ridge security only protected the business and its immediate surroundings—period. The owners didn't care about the rest of the town, which could be rebuilt. The brewery itself was an irreplaceable operation, worth defending to the bitter end.

Everyone else froze, nervously eyed each other, then rushed outside. I figured some of them would want to fight. Others would run. Both options had their appeal.

What to do? What to do?

I fished out a deck of cards, put my .60-cal Meserkov on the table, and played solitaire. Having seen my fair share of massacres, I realized that the best thing to do was to avoid them outright. When that failed, the next best thing was to hole up with a gun and wait it out.

About thirty minutes in, the bar's pre-War jukebox ran out of paid songs and went quiet. Then came the sounds of heavy weapons fire, screams, and armored vehicles rolling past. The attackers came loaded for bear. While the bar shook, the tough brick building was as safe a hidey-hole as I could expect to find on short notice.

Judging from the exchanges of small arms fire, I figured the attackers were winning. Curious, I holstered my gun and headed upstairs. I passed the second-floor bar and snagged a cold one. While it was dark outside, the flames and explosions lit up the nearby streets well enough to see the invaders.

Hmm. A militia had come to town.

By the end of the Sterility War, there were only four types of large assault forces left in America. The remaining thirteen city-states each had their local armies (with about ten thousand guns each). Corporations, like Myther's Ridge, had private armies that rarely exceeded two thousand. Some of the larger biker gangs could—with the right leader—pull together a few hundred goons.

The militias were the most dangerous.

In these semi-Apocalyptic times, the typical militia was a glorified "cult on wheels" with a charismatic butcher for a leader. Militias attracted followers of varying stripes and fought for their respective goals like the pre-War terrorists of old. They always managed to find old arms caches and heavy vehicles. Then they would rampage across the gentle wastelands for a while—until they either splintered or annoyed someone with enough guns to put 'em down.

Four bikers sped off past the edge of town, amid a shower of tracer round fire. They didn't get far. I looked down at the street and saw an eight-man fire team of militia fucks. Dressed in olive drab BDUs, they lined up a dozen captured bikers, forced them to their knees, then raked them with automatic weapons fire—

"Don't move—!" a gruff voice started to shout, before I whipped around and put a one-shot through his chest (without dropping my beer). The militiaman sailed into the air with a silly look on his dead face. Three of his buddies were moving up behind him, only to get knocked off their feet by his corpse.

They didn't see me run up, beer in hand, and open fire. Two of them died before they could raise their guns. I didn't bother with the third guy, who hit the floor hard and screamed from a busted left shoulder.

Better still, he was about my size.

I hustled downstairs, kicked his antique assault rifle away, and knelt on his bad shoulder. Then I sized up my new "friend." The militiaman was in his early twenties, with a lean build and bad breath. His agonized face was reddened with pain and looked about as smart as my left boot.

"Hi," I grinned as I held my smoking barrel just over his right eye. "Answer a few questions and you get to live. Lie—or stay quiet—and I'll end you. Understand?"

Scared to death, he vigorously nodded.

"Good," I grinned as I gave him a silent toast and sipped my beer. I kept an eye on the door, in case any more of his pals came through. "Who are you guys supposed to be?"

"W-we're the Prohibitors," he replied with a hint of pride.

I paused and frowned. "Never heard of ya. Why are you burning my favorite town?"

"Our holy crusade is to destroy dens of vice," he replied with a tremor in his voice.

Took me a few whiffs to realize he shat himself. A flash of embarrassment skipped across his face, then faded back into healthy terror. I nodded for him to continue.

"T-the only way to make America great again is to destroy places of sin . . . like this one."

"A regular 'Sodom and Gomorrah' thing, huh?" I knowingly asked.

He looked surprised that I knew the story. Well, "Mr. High-And-Mighty" wasn't the only one to ever crack open a bible. Ma taught me religion, history, and demolitions.

"So you're gonna kill everyone here?" I asked. "Even the women and children?"

"Y-yessir," nodded the militiaman. "Evil must be uprooted and cleansed before it can grow and spread."

"And by slaughtering the people here," I continued, "you're gonna make America a better place?"

"Y-yessir."

"What's your leader's name?" I asked.

"Marcellus North," he replied with a fanatic's pride.

I drained my brew.

"Thanks," I nodded, before I smashed the empty bottle across his face. The blow dazed him long enough for me to stand up. A few hard stomps to the windpipe left him in the past tense. I changed clothes, under the quiet assumption that these bastards wouldn't be missed for a while. Between them, I put together a decent (shit-free) uniform.

While I dressed, I wondered if these Prohibitors were interested in securing the town at all. Maybe they'd simply fight their way to the brewery and pour fire on it until they won. Then, once victory was assured, this Marcellus North would stick his swelled head out into the open and give some kind of speech . . .

And I could be there to put a bullet through it.

I'm sure I could find a rifle among the bodies. If I was lucky, I might even be able to whip together a "poor man's silencer" for it.

Once I took North out, all hell would break loose and I could disappear in the chaos. The Prohibitors might splinter as their lieutenants went their separate ways. Or worse, North could end up a martyr, whose murder could turbocharge their cultural genocide. The risks involved made me pause.

I could try to sneak back to my motel room. If it was still in one piece, I could grab the rest of my silver and steal one of their vehicles. Running away (in uniform) might work, if I pretended to chase some fleeing sinner . . .

Then I had a really nasty idea.

I grabbed an assault rifle and headed for the door. I'd need some night vision, a fast cycle, and a few bold bikers. Six would be enough. If we made it out of town, they'd go along with my plan because it was ethical, spiteful, and lucrative.

The heist was simple enough.

Marcellus North was a glorified land pirate with a bullshit cause. He drove up here with the bulk of his rabble and most of his vehicles. Night vision would make their trail easy to backtrack. We'd ride, find their HQ, and torch whatever we didn't steal. Of course, they'd leave guards behind and one of them might make a mayday call.

Fine by me. Assuming these assholes left their women and kids behind, they'd drop everything and rush back. I wanted to burn their food, fuel, munitions, and anything else they needed. With an army this well-equipped, I figured that North had plenty of silver to steal.

Even if I left empty-handed, this was worth the risk.

Dens of vice were vital for a crook like me. Without strategic watering holes (like Vegas or Myther's Ridge), I couldn't recruit, resupply, or hide out. Fuck the "innocent" lives at stake. If these Prohibitor bastards weren't stopped, right here and now, I was out of business.

And I'd rather be dead than retired, which was why I snuck out into the slaughter.

KNOWN ASSOCIATES

I spat blood on Special Agent Lisa Sippon's beige carpet as I limped past her. The pear-bottomed fed killed Lenty and Pulliam with a kitchen knife and some decent moves. She even loosened a few of my teeth before I busted a cookie jar over her head. Normally, I'd put one in her skull and disappear—but tonight's situation was kinda unique. That's why she ended up hog-tied in the living room.

I had questions, starting with why Sippon chose to ruin my fucking life. Cold air blew in through the pair of bullet holes in the front door. When I got here, two hours ago, I could've bluffed my way in. Instead, I rang the bell with my suppressed Kimber .45. When Sippon's young babysitter looked through the peephole, I let her have it.

The fed's two kids saw the body fall and bolted for the side door, where Lenty and Pulliam scooped them up. Murdering innocent kids didn't bother me. Nor did I care about leaving forensic traces. As fucked as I was, prison was the least of my worries.

With a groan, the auburn-haired fed opened her eyes and glared up at me. Then she spotted the babysitter's corpse . . . and her kids. That's when her defiance turned into fear. Having come in through the side door, Sippon was clueless about my most recent murder.

Before she could ask, I nodded over to Torrie and Colin. Drugged to the gills, her son and daughter were in their jammies. Blindfolded, bound, and adorable, they slumped in a far corner. Her eyes drifted to the suppressed handgun in my right hand.

"Okay, Dwight, where'd I mess up?" she asked.

Her casual use of my (real) first name bothered me on so many levels.

"Sorry, Special Agent Sippon. We're not on a first-name basis," I replied before I fed her a hard kick to the ribs. Sippon coughed through the pain, eyed her kids, then read the unforgiving hatred in my eyes.

"How'd you find me?" I asked.

The fed kept her mouth shut. After a few seconds, I racked the Kimber's slide and casually aimed at young Torrie.

"Tendril!" Sippon coughed. "I used Tendril on you."

"And what is that?" I asked. "Some kind of fugitive tracker?"

Sippon nodded. "Enter enough data fragments on someone and it'll put digital 'tendrils' through the Internet, dark web, and everywhere else it can reach," she explained. "Even with your dozens of aliases, it IDed you in about six minutes."

"Who owns it?" I asked.

"The NSA," she reluctantly replied.

I gave her a knowing smile. "Some idiot gave you access to the system?"

Sippon nodded, worried by what I could've done with that intel. After all, I'm (arguably) the best con artist of my generation.

"My access was temporary," warned Sippon. "I couldn't let you in if I wanted to."

I frowned at the fed's lack of imagination. On the fly, my devious mind cooked up eight different Tendril-based cons—none of which required real access.

"I don't give a shit about it," I half-lied. "We're way past that."

I brushed pieces of shattered lamp from her cream-colored couch, sat down, then propped my feet on

Pulliam's corpse. It was a rude thing to do—but I needed Sippon to see that I wasn't messing around.

"By the way, who taught you how to fight?" I achingly asked before I slid a throw pillow under the small of my back. "I didn't think Quantico taught the dirty stuff."

"My uncle was a marine," Sippon winced. "You?"

"Here and there," I shrugged.

I truly needed some painkillers and a double bourbon right now. Bothered by my assorted injuries, I slapped the Kimber across my right thigh.

"You do know that you've killed me, right?" I asked with an even tone.

The fed nodded.

"Good," I said. "Now tell me why."

Sippon eyed the blood-stained carpet, then rolled onto her right side.

"The Doren scam," she replied. "Remember it?"

I gave her a proud smile.

"Friedrich Doren," I paused. "Asshole shipping magnate and arms smuggler extraordinaire. I posed as a buyer and took him for five million euros. So?"

"An undercover Interpol team had already gotten to him," Sippon explained. "One of them was a dear friend of mine. Because of you, Doren double-checked his other buyers. That's when he found a crack in their cover—"

"And killed the entire team." I finished without a lick of sympathy. "Wow. My bad."

The fed's bruised, average-looking face glared up at me.

"So you wanted to find and kill me?" I pressed.

"Yeah," Sippon sighed. "Bureau resources came up blank. Interpol didn't believe you existed. A few months ago, I was briefed on Tendril and given limited access

for an unrelated case. During that time, I got friendly
with a programmer."

"Fucked him for it, eh?"

"*Her*," Sippon corrected me without an ounce of
shame.

"Wow," I blinked with a smile. "So you tapped a
back door into the NSA's new tracking algorithm and
found my real name. Why not have me arrested?"

"Nothing I had on you was admissible in a U.S.
court," replied Sippon. "Even if I could put a case
together, some Homeland prick might've recruited you."

She was probably right.

"You could've killed me on your own time," I
argued.

"But what if I missed?" countered the fed. "You'd
either disappear, have me killed, or both. I wanted you to
get the justice you deserved."

"Some of my marks—like Doren—had it coming,"
I reminded her.

"You've also conned churches, sick families, and
even a children's hospital!" scoffed Sippon. "Innocent
people are broke—even dead—because of you."

She had a point there.

"Well, Special Agent Sippon, I'm sorry about your
friend," I openly lied. "If it puts your mind at ease, I'd
say that you got your vengeance—and then some."

I pulled an autopsy photo of Rayna Greene from my
coat. When I raised it, Sippon's guilty reaction was a bit
of cold comfort. Rayna was one of my best partners. I
trained her myself and had even proposed.

Sadly, it didn't last.

Still, Rayna was riding high in the con game—until
Sippon ratted her out. My love's pretty face was beaten
into an unrecognizable pulp. Rayna's killers carved my
real name across her whip-scarred back. Then they really
made her suffer . . .

All because of Special Agent Sippon.

Once the vengeful fed had my aliases, the bitch went on the dark web. She constructed a half-assed alias, then contacted every surviving mark I ever scammed. Each time, Sippon gave out my info. Then, to make matters worse, she gave up the names (and aliases) of my known associates—and didn't charge a dime for it.

My partners usually had plenty of fake identities and stayed on the move. Such was the price of being a grifter in the digital age. Once Sippon ratted them out, photos and all, they were easy to track.

Then they started dropping like flies.

Some of my more sadistic marks (including Doren) pooled their resources. From what I heard, they sent teams of killers after me and my closest friends. After ducking the first two hits, I started warning my peeps—only to learn of their violent deaths.

Naturally, some of my remaining colleagues connected the dots and went underground. A few tried to kill me outright. But some of them offered to help me end this (including Lenty and Pulliam).

The entire time, I tried to reach Rayna—who didn't know that she was being hunted. Once I handled her funeral arrangements, I decided to go on the offensive.

With a sigh, I dropped the photo and picked up the Kimber.

"Wait!" Sippon pleaded. "Turn yourself in and I can arrange some kind of plea deal—even protection!"

I unscrewed the suppressor and tossed it away. The next shots had to be heard. In this suburban neighborhood, the cops would be here within minutes (even in this weather). Then I stood up and took careful, two-handed aim at her daughter.

"No! *Please!*" the bitch pleaded with tears in her eyes.

"You should've killed Doren, Special Agent Sippon," I scowled with a sad glance at Rayna's photo. "Instead, you killed my family. This makes us even."

"They're just kids!" Sippon shouted as I lowered my weapon and paced toward her. "You want payback? Kill me, Dwight. This isn't their fault! It's mine. *Kill me!*"

I pretended to think it over, then gave her a brutal kick to the stomach. As Sippon gasped for air, I casually double tapped her daughter. With the wind knocked out of her, the fed could only sob while I did the same to her boy.

I didn't run because my situation was hopeless. I had to die: plain and simple. With me in the ground, the retribution killings might stop. Whether they did or didn't, I was done. If the "murder pool" hitters didn't get me, the feds would.

Agent Sippon cried through coughs and snot. My adrenaline faded and my aches intensified. I forced a smile and plopped back down on her couch. After a minute or two, we heard sirens in the distance.

Sippon looked up and saw the resigned look in my eyes. It seemed to make her wonder if she'd be next. I flicked on my lighter, then tossed it at her nice drapes. It landed on the carpet and a fire started. Sippon flailed like a trapped animal. Probably wasn't a good time to tell her that I had her home insurance canceled and her investment accounts emptied.

Anyhow, I hoped she survived this.

Then Special Agent Sippon would have to answer for her crimes. Evidence of her unlawful vendetta was already sent to the appropriate parties. There'd be an arrest, conviction, and a very stiff sentence.

I also arranged for Sippon to do the hardest time there was. Some of my surviving associates had expressed an interest in settling up with anyone financing this bloodbath. Their weapon of choice: a number of lucrative revenge scams (some of which I helped plan).

I wished them the best.

As the flames continued to spread, I pressed the Kimber against my heart. Sippon didn't try to talk me down, which hurt my feelings just a bit. At least I had a hand in my own revenge. Not many dead grifters had it so good.

That last thought put a smile on my face, just before I pulled the trigger—

LIFE TAX

Hidden within a maze of underground tunnels and caverns was a colony of Evaders. Satellite imagery couldn't get a reliable read, as they had lined the place with scanner-blocking alloys. We sent in the nanodrones, which hacked their sensor grid and used it to give us a proper head count.

Excluding pets and cattle, the final count came to 689 biosigns. We had some kind of file on most of them. About a fifth of the Evaders were completely off the archives. My guess? They were born and raised down there.

These sad fools were trying to hide from the Internal Revenue Service: the mighty agency that I've given twenty years and two of my children to. Today, they'd get a top-notch lesson in modern tax enforcement.

Nothing's sweeter than a full-scale audit breach. I had combat air support and the honor of commanding 214 agents. We stormed in unannounced, full of lethal grace and unnerving precision.

The perimeter defenses were a joke. We gunned down eighty-nine armed defenders, dismantled nineteen outdated gun drones, and rounded up the rest of the sheep. As usual, most of them gave up without a fight. A few unarmed idiots tried to run—until they were cornered, beaten down, and cuffed.

Inside of thirty minutes, the last Evaders were collected and dumped into the largest cavern, which might've served as a meeting hall of some kind. I ordered a casualty check. We had thirteen wounded agents. Nine more would go home in body bags (which did nothing for my mood).

It was time for "The Speech." I've given it hundreds of times and it rarely changed. I told the

Evaders that they had all (knowingly or unknowingly) violated federal law by not paying their Life Tax—

I was interrupted by a chubby young thing, who reeked of weed and liberal sensibilities. She stepped up and angrily claimed that, since their colony was under western Ecuador, they shouldn't have to pay income taxes to the United States. My shooters laughed as I gave her a patient sigh. Clearly, they didn't teach world history in this glorified sinkhole.

I explained that, sixty-four years ago, the world's population swelled past eleven billion. Folks were killing each other over every imaginable type of resource. Either through war or environmental collapse, humanity faced certain extinction. To avoid this outcome, the fair-minded leaders of the American government simply took over the world.

An old man hobbled up on a cane and shouted obscenities with a solid Irish brogue. Scarred on the right sight of his face and minus his left arm, he cursed us for the death and misery caused by our designer plagues. The old man then bluntly said that he'd rather be shot dead than to pay "one red cent" of his Life Tax.

I complimented him on his grasp of historical context. Then I shot him dead. Ignoring the screamers, I waited until the old man stopped twitching. As blood and brainy bits poured from his skull, I asked that there be no further interruptions.

Then I holstered my sidearm and went on to explain that, at present, the current population of this planet was at a manageable half-billion. There were no more worries about starvation, environmental woes, or even war. Instead, there was a thriving world-nation with order and economic stability.

I congratulated everyone on their automatic United States citizenship. They could choose to remain here (with the bat feces) or rejoin the outside world. Those who made the latter choice could live anywhere they wanted, without such bygone burdens as passports or free speech.

However, there was one dominant civic obligation. That duty wasn't to vote, since all politicians were now drafted by the government. Nor was it to serve in the military, because prisoners' coercion implants made them more than "willing" to enlist.

Nope, our last remaining civic duty was the Life Tax. Anyone who didn't pay up, to the credit, would be executed, per Section 989891.236920 (Paragraph D) of the Revised American Tax Code.

Murmurs of dread filled the room.

I didn't know how much they knew of the tax, nor did I care. All that mattered was that they paid it within the next three hours. The amount owed was ten thousand credits per person, per year.

I explained that my men accepted any and all forms of payment: credits, antique paper money, livestock, jewels, organs, and even contraband. Multiple Evaders would have to pay any back taxes owed, along with a fine of five thousand credits for each year skipped—

A young man tried to run.

One of my agents nailed him in the spine with a well-placed rifle shot. The idiot hit the ground alive, minus the use of his legs. I ignored his sobbing pleas for mercy and asked the assembled Evaders to please form three lines. Each was given our standard-variety truth serum.

Then the processing began in earnest.

Fifty-nine of them had cred sticks and paid up-front. They got hustled toward one of the smaller caverns. Another 103 claimed assorted goods (from organically grown drugs to family heirlooms). Each item was described and its value calculated on the spot, at fair-market value. Thanks to the serum, we could take them at their word. Movers would be sent in to grab everything when we were done.

But, once in a while, something just had to be retrieved on the spot. An elderly couple used a framed, autographed Elvis photo to pay off their back taxes. They even got an instant tax refund from us, which came to 3.5 million credits. Their good fortune drew gasps of envious shock from the younger scum.

I asked if they'd like to pay off anyone else's taxes. They wisely said, "Hell no!" (in perfect unison, no less). Then they scampered off with the other taxpayers. Those were my kind of people.

After all, that's what the Life Tax was really about: the determination of who was worthy of survival. If you couldn't come up with a measly ten thousand credits a year—or find someone else to pay it for you—then you were just taking up space and finite resources.

During the process, we opened DNA files on any adult offenders who grew up down here. Their taxes were waived for one year, as a courtesy. Thus, another ninety-four people were spared the ugly side of our duties and escorted from the main cavern.

Next, eighty-one child dependents were processed. If their parents or next of kin survived the audit, they would be reunited. Otherwise, the orphans would be raised by the state and enjoy immunity from taxation until they turned eighteen.

Now for the fun part.

There were 262 deadbeats who had very little between themselves and a firing squad. Some opted to sell their organs (from eyes to fingers to kidneys). I radioed for the medics to come on down. Thanks to clean living, another seventy Evaders had their taxes paid in full. Even the spine-shot cripple on the ground avoided execution by giving up his legs (which made sense).

During the organ harvesting, the remaining 192
Evaders grew more desperate. A group of eighteen
attractive ladies weepingly joined our unit as "mascots."
As long as they kept us amused, we'd chip in and pay
their annual Life Taxes for them.

Some forty-seven Evaders had advanced degrees in
useful fields. They'd end up being auctioned off as
servants for corporations in need of cheap labor. While
half of their pitiful wages would be gobbled up by the
tax, they'd be alive to gripe about it.

That left us with 127 wretched Evaders, all of
whom were unfit to survive the audit. Their pleas for
mercy fell on our deaf, bureaucratic ears. As my men
herded them along the main cavern's lengthy eastern
wall, I saw that we had eighteen minutes to spare.

Normally, it would've taken us an extra hour to
process so many sheep. Such efficiency made me feel
proud to be a civil servant in this new global America.
Feeling oddly magnanimous, I asked if anyone wanted a
blindfold or a smoke. We always had surpluses of both
but rarely bothered to offer them up.

Eighty-four Evaders slipped on blindfolds. A dozen
of my agents provided cheap lighters to those who
wanted a last smoke. Only a few of them showed any
shred of dignity in the face of certain death. The rest
simply broke down and sobbed. Enviously, I looked on
as twenty of my subordinates aimed their rifles.

Just as I was about to give the kill order, three of
my agents brought in a late arrival. This one was a
skinny man in a black-and-red dress of some kind. In his
early eighties, his outfit had a weird white thing in his
collar and some kind of brown-beaded belt around his
waist.

Unfamiliar with the uniform, I folded my arms and
told them to report. His name was Cardinal Tavin
Shawkle. The frail fellow belonged to something called

the "Catholic Church." In the name of "God," he begged me to spare these people's lives.

God . . . The name sounded vaguely familiar.

I had one of my tax historians pull up the background profile. Before the U.S. took over the world and abolished religion, government policy was influenced by an extinct subcaste known as "clergy." They worshipped imaginary beings, held significant political power, and opposed most forms of progress (based on outdated moral platforms).

When America's leaders saved the world, the global religious community stubbornly resisted. In the end, they even attempted to spur the remaining population to rebel, which resulted in the Great Purge of 2111. Fed up with holy folks, the government slaughtered them wholesale.

All traces of their existence were either destroyed or confiscated by the state. To this day, any surviving priest, nun, rabbi, imam, et cetera was to be deemed a traitor and executed in the name of national security.

Fine by me.

I removed Father Shawkle's wire-rimmed glasses (which looked valuable), then socked him in the nose. My agents grinned at the awkward way in which he fell. I drew my sidearm and aimed for the heart. In obvious pain, Shawkle held up his hands and begged for thirty seconds of my time. Well, even with the blindfolds and smokes, we were ahead of schedule . . .

I gave him the nod. Shawkle explained that, under federal law, we had to let the Evaders go and refund whatever they paid us. When we stopped laughing (and it took us a while), I asked Father Shawkle what narcotic substance helped him reach that bizarre conclusion.

The cardinal pointed out that we were standing in a church. Under current federal law, churches couldn't be taxed. Shawkle reached into his dress and pulled out a laminated document. Pre-dating the Purge, it detailed how the "Pope" had several global sites registered as *American* churches.

This dry toilet was one of them.

I wanted to end him so badly that my trigger finger involuntarily twitched. However, rules were rules. With five minutes left, I lowered my gun and had the claim verified. My historians ran the document through the departmental databases and the damned thing turned out to be legit. No one bothered to seize this particular "church" before the confiscation cycle ended.

Even worse, there was an old federal law about churches being tax-exempt. For some reason, it wasn't taken off the books. There was even some post-Purge legislation, which stated that residents and dependents of a Church couldn't be taxed either. That they were, in effect, "clergy" themselves.

Congress!

Even without parties, they'd legalize anything for the right price! I grudgingly holstered my sidearm and told Father Shawkle that he should've been a lawyer. The once-doomed Evaders cheered as I gave my firing squad the order to stand down. I helped Shawkle to his feet, returned the glasses, and praised him for his courage and quick thinking.

Then I pulled up a monitor and looked for a precedent. As luck would have it, another entry team ran into one of these "Cavern Churches," in Old Israel, some ten years ago. The IRS agent-in-charge documented his actions, which were later approved by the Treasury Department.

I reviewed what he did, muttered a profanity, then asked Shawkle if everyone here was affiliated with this Church. He eagerly confirmed that they were. I had them all rounded up in the main hall, where I told them that they were immune to the Life Tax (for now).

Then I ordered my team to pack it up. The audit movers were late (as usual), so their contraband and other valuables were safe. Since organs and creds were taken, we couldn't just refund without due process. With a straight face, I offered paper copies of the AJ-25-6231.88 Reimbursement Forms. Some of my agents snickered in the background because the typical turnaround was about thirty-six years.

Our thirty dropships descended and picked us up. As we left, the pair of elderly Elvis fans approached me. Rich enough to live anywhere, they were afraid that their fellow cave dwellers might hold a grudge. Yes, Darwin would've been proud.

I insisted that they fly out with me.

As soon as we were in the air, I grabbed a headset and informed the dropship pilots that there was an ordained priest down there. Seeing as he was a traitor and a threat to national security, unlimited force was authorized, per IRS tactical precedent. The folks who stayed behind were "aiding and abetting" this traitor and thus deserved no protection under current law—even the children.

I ordered them to use the nerve gas first, then the penetration ordinance. Out of some sense of misguided guilt, the wealthy ex-Evaders begged me to show mercy. I politely told them to shut up or die.

Then, in the name of world stability, I gave the order to attack . . .

NEIGHBORHOOD WATCH

Deidre Nattens and her son Kyle ran through the fog-shrouded night in shared terror. Just over thirty, the long-haired brunette was beautiful in her black formal dress. Even in heels, she moved with a desperate, athletic grace.

Somehow Kyle managed to keep stride. A head shorter than his mother, the lanky thirteen-year-old wore a brown suit, white shirt, and black necktie. His blond hair and grayish eyes were from his father but he had his mother's face.

After several long minutes, they stopped at a familiar street. Both winded and hungry, they anxiously looked around.

"Where do we go?" Kyle asked amidst panicked gulps of air.

Deidre took a step and stumbled as her left shoe heel broke. She angrily removed her shoes and weighed their options. They used to live around here. Some of their old neighbors should still be around. One of them would take them in.

They had to!

Deidre took her son's hand and ran toward Mencer Street.

Exactly twenty seconds later, a pair of black Durango SUVs rushed out of the fog and screeched to a halt. Virgil Muhes jumped out of the lead vehicle and stood within its low beams. With him were six other gangbangers—all in their early- to late-twenties. Called "The Trigger Happies," they ran this neighborhood and didn't have a problem shooting anyone who thought otherwise. They warily spread out with guns drawn.

Virgil lowered his modified AK-47 with an anxious scowl. He was a "lieutenant" of sorts, with responsibilities that included folks like Deidre and Kyle. Huge and black, Virgil looked down and spotted her discarded shoes.

His cell phone pinged. Virgil pulled it with his left hand. On the screen was a short text with Deidre's and Kyle's full names listed . . . and an old address.

"They on Mencer," he said with tobacco-stained teeth. "Split off and squeeze 'em in. I got the middle."

His crew hopped into the SUVs and drove off. Virgil ran toward Mencer Street. Deidre grew up in this neighborhood, then blew town after college. A few years ago, she moved back in to take care of her mom.

At least, that's what Deidre told everyone. Street gossip was that she moved her son away from an abusive ex. Virgil strained to remember her mom's name . . .

Rudek. Old Mrs. Rudek. With the name came memories of a yellow, two-story house. The gangbanger remembered Halloween trick-or-treat runs and how old Mrs. Rudek used to hook him up. Then again, Virgil also remembered stealing her car when he was in high school. Now, the old lady was dead—and he was hell-bent on gunning down her only daughter and grandchild.

*   *   *

Deidre led Kyle past her mom's house, which still had a FOR SALE sign in front. She stopped, anxiously looked around at the other houses, and noted that their lights were all off.

"Let's go inside!" Kyle pleaded as he pointed to his grandmother's house.

"It's the first place they'd look," Deidre reasoned. "Let's try Jim's place."

Kyle nodded as he wiped a thin sheen of sweat from his brow. Four houses away was a well-maintained gray home. They reached the steps and Deidre desperately rang the bell while Kyle pounded on the metal-barred screen door. A light came on upstairs. Precious seconds slipped past. The door opened and a very sleepy Jim Oshroe appeared. Tall and chubby, the sixtysomething retiree narrowed his nearsighted eyes and flipped on his porch light.

"Jim!" Deidre smiled with relief. "Thank God you're home! Please let us in!"

When Oshroe recognized them, his eyes widened with fear–

Then he slammed the door shut, just before Virgil rushed into view and fired from the hip. Kyle spun into an eight-round burst to the face and torso. Deidre saw her son go down, sprouted fangs, and angrily rushed Virgil with inhuman speed. Most of his shots either missed or grazed the vampire.

Fortunately, Virgil came prepared. He gave the assault rifle's metal buttstock a quick twist. Out snapped a sharpened oak stake. With practiced ease, Virgil "butt-staked" Deidre through the heart.

Still, she slammed into him with such force that they both went down. Virgil spun with the impact and landed atop the vampire's dying frame. He didn't risk stabbing her again. Nor did he feed her the rest of the mag. No, the gangbanger simply kept his weight down on the stake.

Too weak to fight or even move, Deidre glared up at him for a seeming eternity. Then her eyes closed as she died again. Only then did Virgil rip his weapon free and empty the mag into Deidre's beautiful face—just to be sure. The hybrid wood-and-metal ammo was specially made to lodge inside of a target.

His posse arrived at the scene and lowered their guns.

"Heads," Virgil muttered as he reloaded and looked around.

A few of the house lights came on but no one would call the police. They knew better. Virgil shook off his collision with the vampire and eyed his stake—which was still dry. Relieved, the gangbanger twisted the AK again and made it retract.

Two of Virgil's guys drew machetes and proceeded to behead Deidre and Kyle. Neither corpse bled—either from the gunshot wounds, the stake, or even the beheadings. That meant these two hadn't fed yet, which was more luck than anything else. Julio (Virgil's number two) slipped a cigarette into his worried mouth and fired it up.

"How the fuck they get past us?" Julio asked with a slight Puerto Rican accent.

Virgil didn't answer because he had no idea. Usually, the local coroners and funeral homes let them know when a vamp-related homicide came up. He'd secure the corpse, wait for the internal organs to grow back, then ask a few questions. When it was done, the vamp always got "re-killed" and returned to the mortician.

Somehow, these two slipped through the cracks.

Little Bo was banging some Goth chick in the cemetery, when Deidre broke out of her grave. By the time the vampire unearthed her son, Bo had it called in. If the newly risen pair found a decent hiding place, they could've turned a dozen people—*in their 'hood*—by week's end.

"This shit was intentional," said Tre, an overly tatted white guy with a thin blond beard. "Too bad they can't tell us who bit 'em."

One of the other Trigger Happies unfolded two black body bags. After eighty-plus kills (most of them vamps), Virgil felt a bit guilty about Deidre and Kyle. Whatever turned them deserved a slow, hard death—and he meant to personally deliver it.

"Put the word out," the gang lieutenant commanded with a quiet menace. "I want twenty-four-seven eyes on our streets: especially where we're soft. And warn the other gangs to watch their graveyards. Until this is handled, we're at war."

"Stick or carrot?" Julio asked as he pulled a burner phone, ready to free up bribe money or torture rooms on his leader's command.

"Muthafuckin' stick," Virgil glared. "Grab anyone who got near these two in the last month. The drunk who wrecked their car. The ex-husband. The pallbearers who put them in the hearse. *Every-fucking-body!* Hurt 'em all until the blanks are filled. Then we get messy."

Grins formed among the more sadistic members of his posse.

"You sure about this, *hommes*?" Julio hesitated. "A war's bad for business."

"What if the next vamps find your girls?" Tre countered.

Julio's face darkened as Deidre and Kyle were zipped up. Then, he glanced over at Virgil, who gave him the nod. With a sigh, Julio raised the phone to his ear and started a war.

SPECIAL AGENT

This was the fifth murder in three days.

The culprit was an audacious nut job who placed a branded left thumbprint on the forehead of each victim. How'd he burn it into his victims? Forensics was still working that angle.

While the print wasn't in the system, he left enough evidence for an easy conviction. The killer was a redheaded white male, left-handed, about five-ten, with a size twelve shoe. All we had to do was catch the bastard.

His M.O. was consistent with a semi-pro trying to show off—either to the public, the police, or to someone in particular. He didn't appear to take any trophies from the victims or leave us weird clues (aside from the thumbprint). Nor were there signs of sexual violence or torture.

This one always killed quickly, then fled the scene. No witnesses have ever come forward. Nor did any of the vics appear to have a single goddamned thing in common. He didn't even kill 'em the same way.

His first victim, a machinist, was hit by a stolen car. The killer parked the front tires across the body then abandoned the vehicle.

The next morning, he slit a huge biker's throat with a straight-edged razor and no signs of a struggle. The same day, just after recess, he slipped into a grade school and strangled a six-year-old girl in a hallway. No one saw shit.

Later that evening, the killer broke into a retired librarian's home and sent her down a flight of basement stairs. Forensics thinks her neck snapped during the fall. Me? I wasn't so certain.

What was the significance of three kills in one day? We couldn't agree on a working theory. The fifth victim's death really livened things up. Last night, he drowned Judge Silvia Hallam in her tub. Her husband was sleeping in the next room. Both kids were downstairs with the family dog. Even though Judge Hallam put up a fight, no one saw or heard a thing. Forensics found the killer's hair, skin, and blood under her fingernails. His signature thumbprint was placed on the judge's forehead, just like the others. I was starting to wonder if Hallam was the real target, with the other kills thrown in for misdirection.

Some of my superiors had the same thought. Overnight, high-level meetings were held about a plan of attack. We expected the feds to claim jurisdiction.

This morning, Fykes and I were pulled aside. We were told to pick up some FBI consultant from the downtown Greyhound station. Aside from offering every courtesy, we were to get him to the morgue ASAP. Between the traffic and summer construction, we made it a few minutes late.

As soon as we parked, Special Agent Roy Coltry stepped up. The department texted us his photo, which did him justice. Then there was the trademark (blue) FBI windbreaker he had on. The bald-shaven consultant wore a plain black Kevlar vest under the windbreaker, with no apparent sidearm. He looked somewhere in his late forties with a black metal band around his right thumb.

Blue-eyed and tired-looking, the fed wasn't that tall but he clearly hit the gym. Weighing two-twenty or so, he could've been an athlete or a former vet. A pair of passing grandmas checked him out as they passed.

"Why's a fed riding Greyhound?" Fykes asked. "Don't they have cars of their own?"

I simply shrugged. Most feds weren't all that bad. Granted, some were ambitious, backstabbing assholes with delusions of talent. Then there were the damaged weirdoes who shouldn't be wearing a badge, which this guy might've been.

With a forced smile, I lowered the window.

"Detectives Fykes and Gryshoisky?" he asked (without butchering my last name).

"Yep," I replied. "Special Agent Coltry?"

"Reporting for duty," replied the fed. When Fykes popped the door locks, Coltry opened the back door of our sedan.

The fed tossed the duffel bag inside and got in behind me. He pulled his credentials and flashed them before I could ask. I briefly checked his ID then handed it back.

"You waitin' on any luggage?" Fykes asked as Coltry closed the door.

"Nope," replied the fed. "Please head for 9821 Pensetter Avenue."

Fykes shrugged and started driving. Pensetter was on the way to the morgue, but that wasn't the point.

"Um, we're supposed to bring you in to review the latest case," I politely reminded him.

"Yeah. That's not gonna happen," Coltry casually replied. "Mind if I smoke?"

Fykes, health nut that he was, semi-glared at the rearview. "Knock yourself out."

"Thanks," Coltry smiled as he reached into his bag and produced a small wooden case. Inside was a white, hand-carved ivory smoking pipe and what looked to be four unmarked tobacco tins.

"That's one way to manage your habit," I grinned as he chose a tin and unscrewed it.

"It helps me focus during the critical points of a case," confided the agent.

We stopped at a light as Coltry courteously lowered his window, packed the pipe, and pulled an old Zippo lighter from his gray jeans. He lit up and the car smelled like that quality shit my grandpa used to smoke.

"So, what's at Pensetter?" Fykes asked with an impatient edge.

"The next crime scene," Coltry replied with a straight face. "If we hurry, we might save the poor guy."

Good thing there weren't any cars behind us as the light turned green. Still in the intersection, Fykes turned around with a disbelieving scowl.

"Come again?" balked my partner.

The fed buckled up. "You drive. I'll talk. And no sirens—please."

"Floor it," I sighed.

To his credit, Fykes hit the gas.

I figured Coltry fell into the category of "weirdo fed," which meant that I'd have to keep him from fucking up this case. To do that, I needed to know what he knew. I opened my mouth to ask about—

"The intended vic is Carlos Eduardo Hortiz: age fifty-nine," Coltry began as he eyed our dashboard clock. "He's a security guard, whose shift ended about nine minutes ago. The killer's waiting for him in the parking deck across the street."

Fykes glanced at me through his wire-rimmed glasses. My long-time partner's silent message was simple enough: *we need to call this in.* I figured that if we didn't listen (and Hortiz ended up dead), it would be our asses. If this tip was bullshit, we'd get chewed out for being late—which I could live with. What we couldn't do was call down the world: not without being sure.

My partner hit some side streets and got us to Pensetter Avenue without any collisions. Along the way, Coltry took off his windbreaker and read the tension on Fykes' face.

"Call it in, if you want," said the agent, as he puffed away on his pipe. "We just need to come in quiet and normal. Then head for the third level. I don't want to spook him."

"Who are we looking for?" Fykes asked as he ran a red light. It was a dumb question—unless my partner was testing Coltry. After five murders, we already knew the bastard's ethnicity, hair color, and approximate height.

Coltry looked past us.

"A red-haired, Caucasian male with a dorky face," he replied. "Early twenties, five-ten, and about a buck ninety. He'll be wearing a white pair of Adidas street sneakers, blue jeans, and a striped white-and-yellow Polo shirt."

The detail of the description was beyond eerie— especially the killer's age and "dorky" face.

"That's one helluva source," I replied with a curious frown as I reached for the radio.

"Guess you could say that," Coltry muttered, before he stuffed his windbreaker into the bag. "We won't need backup just yet."

"What's this guy's name?" I asked.

I set the radio down.

"Don't know or care," admitted our passenger. "All that matters is that Mr. Hortiz is about to die on the second level of a parking garage."

Fykes slowed down as we approached the three-level structure.

The pipe still in his mouth, Coltry removed his Kevlar vest—maybe to blend in. We rolled up to the parking deck and stopped at its entrance barrier. Fykes angrily ripped the machine's white parking stub and rolled through as its gray barrier went up.

"What's Hortiz driving?" I asked.

"He won't make it to his car," replied Coltry as he grabbed a fed-issue body cam from his bag and clipped it to his belt, near the buckle. "Please slow down, Detective Fykes."

"What's the plan?" I asked.

The fed stared past me again as we rolled toward the second level.

"Stop here," Coltry ordered.

Fykes hit the brakes with an irritated sigh. Coltry opened the door then anxiously looked around.

"Head for Level Three and park next to the yellow Hummer," ordered the fed. "Once you park, *then* call for backup—and come down with guns drawn."

"What about Hortiz?" Fykes asked.

Coltry stepped out with his bag. "You'll pass him on the way down. Again, act normal—because he's the bait. Otherwise, the killer disappears. Questions?"

Coltry had rank and there wasn't time to argue this.

"Understood," I sighed, glad that my pension was locked in.

With a parting nod, Agent Coltry slung the bag over his right shoulder and turned to leave.

"Need a piece?" I reluctantly asked with a low voice.

"Not this time," Coltry replied, then closed the door with a casual menace.

Fykes and I swapped angry glances. Coltry was using a civilian as bait, which wasn't right. There should've been a lockdown around this entire neighborhood—especially if the feds knew this bastard's face.

Still, I pulled my piece and kept it low. Good thing too, because that's when *we passed the intended murder victim.*

"Jesus!" Fykes gasped as he eyed the rearview.

Carlos Eduardo Hortiz had his earbuds on and both eyes on his smartphone. Totally in his own little world, the poor bastard didn't even notice us pass him. A navy-blue security uniform and matching cap covered his stocky frame. Hortiz was a graying, off-duty schmuck just looking to go home—easy pickings for our killer.

I checked my gun.

"See anyone else?" Fykes anxiously asked.

"No," I muttered.

"Where's Coltry getting his intel?" whispered my partner.

"I dunno. Maybe his snitch was at the bus station," I shrugged. "Everything he's said's been right, so far. Just stick with his script and be ready to call it in."

"This fucker's nuts!" Fykes bristled as we reached the third level. "How'd he even know about a . . . ?"

Our jaws dropped at the sight of a yellow Hummer and a vacant parking space next to it. That's when our last doubts about Coltry went away.

"Call it in!" I snapped.

My partner nodded, then stopped to let me out.

Lucky for me I was in my comfy loafers. I raced for the nearest stairs. At my age, the trick to keeping decent knees was *not to run*. Hours on the stationary bike didn't erase my gut but it did wonders for my stamina. The adrenaline—plus having to explain away a dead fed—put me on the second level in under ten seconds.

As I flung aside the stairwell door, Hortiz stopped just short of my gun barrel. The vic quivered in fear with his bloodied right hand clamped over a nasty gash on his left arm. I lowered my piece and flashed my badge.

"Get in the third-floor stairwell and stay put!" I whispered. "My partner's right behind me."

Scared shitless, the balding guard ran past me and straight for the stairs. Good. I rushed out of the stairwell, spotted Hortiz's blood trail, and looked for—

The killer was kicked into my line of view. He fell past a parked van and landed hard. Coltry's description was a spot-on match: except for the *knife in his chest*. It was lodged in the killer's sternum, all the way to the hilt. Yet the kid was already back to his feet, pissed as hell.

Why wasn't he dead?

Coltry angrily stormed toward the killer as I assumed a shooter's stance. The fed closed in too fast for me to risk a shot. I shouted for the killer to halt . . . then noticed an impossible lack of sound: like I suddenly went deaf or something.

Coltry nailed the bastard with a brutal left cross to the jaw. Normal blood flew from the young bastard's mouth, only to *crumble* as it hit the deck. Like it turned solid in mid-fall! I started to question my sanity as Coltry ripped the large hunting knife from the killer's chest.

More blood gushed from the wound but turned solid too. The killer reacted with a silent shriek of agonized rage—which made no sense. This prick should be dead by now. There should be sounds all around me: from my breathing to passing traffic.

Instead, there was only silence.

The psycho threw a desperate haymaker. Coltry easily blocked it and sliced the kid (maybe) eight times. I've seen enough martial arts demos to know what the fed meant to do. Every slash and thrust was along an artery or through a vital organ.

Coltry then stepped away, absolutely certain this fight was over. The killer stumbled back with a defiant smile . . . before he collapsed into a pile of wax-like pieces. Like someone rigged a human piggy bank to break apart for a commercial.

Only his head stayed intact. I watched it bounce away behind a parked Lexus. Then everything sounded normal again. Needing many drinks, I cautiously approached.

"Clear," Coltry confirmed, covered in sweat and a bit out of breath. The thick scent of burning candle wax filled the air around us as I lowered my piece.

"You all right?" I asked.

The fed nodded. Most people get cut up in knife fights. Being both unarmed and against a serial killer, Coltry should've been covered in blood—both his and the killer's. Other than bruised knuckles, the fed didn't have a mark on him.

I'd wager that Coltry was more skilled than lucky. Even the agent's body cam was still on him. Something told me I'd never get to see the raw footage.

"Case closed," Coltry sighed.

"How do we write this up?" I griped. "Even a Santa-loving child wouldn't believe this story!"

"No worries," assured the fed, who went looking for the head. "Expect the FBI to take over from here."

Coltry ducked between two parked cars and collected the unusual piece of evidence. The damned thing looked like the head of a violently murdered wax statue. Even the "blood" on its face was wax.

"But how the fuck do we explain this?" I asked.

"Just tell the basic facts, Detective," grinned the fed. "I came in with an anonymous tip and—thanks to your timely assist—caught the killer red-handed. He escaped, I'll sketch out a description, then nothing."

"You wanna make this a cold case," I frowned. "You really think that'll fly?"

"Leave out what you saw here and it might even fool your partner," Coltry smirked. "Don't worry. The federal government's pretty good at cover-ups."

The way he said it reminded me that the FBI had the resources to bury this. If I stepped out of line, they could do the same to my career. God! I needed a drink right now.

"Do it right, Coltry," I warned him. "Now, why the thumbprint? Tell me that, at least."

"Hold this," he ordered, after a moment's hesitation.

I holstered my piece. Agent Coltry handed me the killer's head. Close-up, I saw the "likeness" of a nerdy young scumbag with a seemingly innocent face. That thought shook me back to the ridiculous reality of this situation. I was holding a wax head covered in wax blood. If not for the bodies in the morgue, I couldn't take this seriously at all.

Coltry grimly walked around a parked Jeep and spotted his duffel bag. With a satisfied smile, the fed unfastened his body cam and dropped it in. The whole time I just stood there, wax head and all.

"Check the back of his neck," said the agent.

I turned the head over and saw a single thumbprint.

"It's different than the one on the victims," Coltry explained.

"Whoever made this 'thing' left his print on purpose?" I guessed.

"It's a calling card, a challenge, or an escalation," Coltry reasoned. "Hopefully, we can figure that out as we track the wax sculptor."

I didn't envy the legwork involved in narrowing down this fucker. Granted, making wax sculptures shouldn't be a thriving art. Certain supplies and materials were required—shit the feds could track faster than we could. Finding this rat bastard was one thing. Turning this into a legit case for the courts would be next to impossible . . .

Unless 'Special' Agent Coltry wasn't looking for an arrest.

Maybe he was a hitman for the feds, sent to solve cases that could never see trial. That explained his discreet entrance and lack of a (traceable) gun. I was only seeing the tip of an iceberg here. While I was curious about the wax sculptor's rationale, the survivor in me didn't wanna look any deeper.

Coltry retrieved his pipe from the hood of a white Impala. He reverently emptied the tobacco then put it back in its case. After the agent dropped it in the duffel bag, he held it under the killer's head. I took the hint and carefully placed it inside. For the first time, I got a good look at the rest of the bag's contents.

Inside were three wrapped sandwiches, two bottled waters, and a spare body cam. Stranger still was the stuff he didn't have in there. The fed didn't pack toiletries, a gun, spare ammo, or even a clean pair of undies. It was like he expected this indefinite, citywide homicide investigation to end by dinner.

The agent's eyes narrowed at the sight of my red button-down shirt.

"Detective, how often do you wear your vest?" Coltry asked with a worried smile, as we both heard sirens in the distance.

"Only when I'm on duty. Why?"

"Three days from now, at six-twelve in the evening," he warned, "you'll walk in on an armed robbery at the Shinehouse Liquor Shack. You'll take three to the chest."

He paused to let that sink in.

"Fykes will get the perp," Coltry added, "but you'll be dead before the ambulance arrives."

I wanted to ask how he knew this . . . then I finally understood why the feds sent him. Somehow, Coltry could see the future. Nothing else made sense. His intel was just too precise: from the killer's description to that yellow Hummer. If that was the case, I was a dead man in three days.

The fed walked past me with a thoughtful smile.

"I think your partner's looking for you," Coltry nodded.

"I'll bet," I muttered as Fykes stepped out with Hortiz in tow. The guard looked pained, yet relieved to be alive.

"Speaking of beers, Special Agent Coltry . . ." I started to offer, when I turned around and found him gone.

Also missing were his duffel bag and every trace of our shattered killer: wax pieces and all. Only Coltry's discarded tobacco and the bloody knife remained. When the first patrol cars approached, I held up my badge.

Once I finished the paperwork on this case, I'd tip off Robbery-Homicide about the Shinehouse robbery. Then I'd call in sick for the next three days—just to be sure.

SUPER DRUNK

In desperate need for some Bacardi, I belly crawled toward the bar while red plasma streams whizzed past me. Everyone else was dying, dead, or huddled under the banquet tables. Anyone who fled for an exit didn't get very far.

There were many reasons not to marry—and wedding receptions nearly topped the list. Sloppy and puerile, I preferred bachelor parties or even funerals. What made this reception different was that assorted super villains decided to crash the party. They left the second-rate minions and freelance scum at home.

These were heavy hitters. Some I recognized by name. Others might've been up-and-comers or before my time. Either way, they carried themselves like villainous All-Stars.

Like most heroes, Mom and Dad were smart enough to conceal their secret identities. Sizer wasn't so discreet (or smart). The Samoan was a quarter-ton of muscled perfection, who could crush diamonds like they were cookies. Needless to say, his god-like strength saved billions of lives (mine included).

Vanity was his only flaw.

Wife Number Four got it into Sizer's head to "out" himself and get paid. So he wrote an autobiography and sold his movie rights. Dwayne "The Rock" Johnson agreed to play the lead, even if he was a bit too small for the part.

Yet, Sizer mistakenly thought he could have a safe, private wedding. Then again, I was stupid enough to accept the big idiot's invitation to this surprise bloodbath. Had to admit: it's the most interesting reception I'd ever been to.

Last I saw, someone put an electrified crossbow bolt through the bride's perfect ears. Killed "Steve Martin" style, her funeral would warrant a giggle or two.

As for Sizer? The poor guy barely lasted five seconds into the fight before he seized up and fell over. The apparent cause of death was poison, which anyone could've slipped into his food or drink. A designer toxin would be the easiest way to kill a guy who once waded through an artillery barrage to save a former president.

Adios, big guy.

But that wasn't the worst of it. The villains expected Sizer's fellow supers to be present. If they were wrong, so be it. If they were right, then some of the guests-slash-heroes might fight back.

The heroic response was less than perfect. Some of them were cut down with the other guests. A few others tried to fight back. Rather than watch them die, I used the time they bought me.

Good thing I was drinking champagne earlier. Most vintages made me a genius. I had a few glasses earlier, mainly to get into the panties of a hot Jamaican bartender across the room. Now that it was in my system, my IQ was off the charts.

My "liquid genius" allowed me to estimate that my parents would die within the next ninety seconds. Mom and Dad were old-school heroes. They'd find a quiet corner and costume up. From what I could see, they were outnumbered but only slightly outpowered.

Dad's nanomorphic implant allowed him to turn into a faceless, crystalline brute. Once in that form, he could create small, ultratech devices. With Sizer dead, Dad was the strongest hero in the room.

But if he stepped out, he'd lose. Three of the hostiles had psi-guns that could fry his mind. One was a mystic, with spells that could end him too. As for the rest . . . Dad might hold his own.

Then there was Mom. A multi-billionaire inventor, she fell victim to a rare and stubbornly degenerative disease. Even with champagne in my blood, I couldn't devise a cure. To survive, she chose to replace key organs with cyberware and asked Dad for help (which was how they met).

Not only did the cyberware keep Mom alive, it allowed her to get pregnant with my sorry ass. While fifty-eight, she looked twenty years younger with an Amazonian physique that caught every straight man's eye (except mine, of course). The cyberware left Mom fast and strong—just not in Dad's league. Still, put a weapon in her hand and she was legendary. Back-to-back, they might take twenty-six or so baddies with them, leaving another dozen to run wild.

I reached the bar and found some Bacardi Rum. With shaking hands, I unscrewed the cap and ducked behind the bar. That cute Jamaican gal's face was half-missing, courtesy of a well-thrown plasmarang.

I closed my eyes as shattered glass rained down past my face and rental tux. Then I took a hefty plug of Barcadi . . . and froze time. The world didn't really stop—just everyone and everything within this modest-sized banquet hall. My watch still ticked and I noted the time because this effect lasted (precisely) six minutes.

Bacardi in hand, I slowly rose and carefully strode over to the parental units. This "time-stop" thing's got two flaws. First, if I try this shit more than three times a day, I'll have a truly painful micro-stroke. Second, if I move too quickly, time instantly resumes its normal flow in here. Even with the champagne genius, I don't know why.

It took me a minute to reach my folks, who were frozen mid-argument. Hard to believe they stuck together for thirty-one years (this June). Dad was carefree and Mom was hyper-anal. They had nothing in common but me and crimefighting.

Oh, right. They loved each other way too much.

I set the bottle down, touched my parents, and undid the time freeze effect.

"What the hell?!" they practically yelped in unison.

"No sudden moves," I warned them. "Or this field drops and more people die."

My parents stared at me like I asked them to vote Republican. Then they took in the carnage and slowly nodded.

"You could stop time all along?!" Dad whispered with shocked paternal pride.

"Only when I drink Bacardi," I winked. "And you don't have to whisper. They're all frozen for about five more minutes."

"Your super power's alcohol-based?" Mom frowned.

Knowing her, she was scanning every inch of me, unsure of how she had missed it. Dad's powers came from an alien abduction, which meant I should've been born a super. As a kid, they wanted me to step up and get into the hero game.

When I came out normal, they were a bit disappointed. I was too—until I had my first wine cooler (and realized I could read minds).

"This wasn't just a hit on Sizer," I explained. "It's also a fishing expedition for heroes. Who's left?"

My parents looked for possible allies in the carnage . . . then their faces fell.

"It's just us and civilians," Mom replied. "What's the plan?"

Dad and I swapped shocked reactions at the deferential question. See? I'm a loser. That's my secret identity. I had three DUIs, thinning hair, and a basement apartment. I'd done temp work for years, ever since I dropped out of college. That's when Mom kicked me out of the mansion.

I maintained a resentful façade and treated them like dirt. All the while, I made billions on Wall Street. I also surfed the dark web and quietly thwarted eighteen individual attempts on my parents' lives. All of this shit was thanks to different brands of alcohol and the assorted powers they gave me.

"Teleportation studs," I grinned.

Dad chuckled, nodded, then willed his right hand into nanocrystal.

"How many?" he asked.

Mom pulled a quick scan. "I count thirty-eight hostiles. Make it seventy . . . to account for the wounded."

Dad flipped his crystalline palm downward and slowly ran it across the floor. Dime-sized tech poured out, in a straight line, for the next two minutes.

"How many trips can those things make?" I asked.

"Two," Dad replied.

"All right," Mom nodded with narrowed eyes. "Interfacing with each stud . . . Targeting the severely wounded and each of the bad guys . . . Done."

"Jail for one group and the nearest hospitals for everyone else," Dad urged.

Mom shook her head.

"They killed our friends to send a message," she scowled. "I'm sending one back. What's the range? Nine miles up, right?"

Dad nodded, bothered by the look in Mom's eye. Maybe he had just realized that most of these maniacs couldn't fly. Fair enough. If any of them survived the fall, I'm certain that my parents could deal with them later.

"Wait for me to get back to the bar," I cautioned them. "Then move to your exact positions. Once you send the studs, time will resume. Play "human" and get out."

Dad nodded with a wink and a smile. I started to make my way back.

"And son?" Mom called out.

"Yeah?" I asked.

"When this is over, we're gonna have a *long* talk about your future," she vowed.

"Sure, Ma," I grinned with my back to her. "Whatever you say."

When this was over, I'd need to drink a frozen chocolate margarita to edit their memories of this shitty night. Then a bourbon chaser to psi-hack into Mom's cyberware and delete our little conversation from her internal drives.

If they wanted to be heroes and save the day, fine. All I wanted to be was a happy survivor with the world at my feet. I wouldn't let anything as trivial as the "civic good" ruin that.

THAT WAS FUN

I sipped my beer in front of a stunning Pacific sunset. At my feet was a solid gold cooler. Packed with ice, it came with four chilled beers inside. Unable to find a decent beach chair, I sprawled out on the sand in my gray tac armor. Some poor schmuck's corpse made for a decent pillow.

As I adjusted my tinted goggles, there was a crashing sound to the north. I looked over, just in time to see Francisco de la Dante's mountainous compound collapse in on itself. The sight of it was the most triumphant moment of my life.

The late mastermind had built this dome-shaped, ultratech lair on an uncharted island. Well off the shipping lanes, it was ringed with ultratech defenses and manned by about six hundred competent minions. Poor ol' Dante thought he was untouchable.

Until we came along, maybe he was right.

Over twenty-plus years, Dante systematically acquired power through an ever-growing cartel. The quality of his resources and scumbags improved over the years, to the point where he might've ruled the world someday. His winning strategy was to find those with influence and discreetly control it.

It seemed simple enough but it wasn't. Stealing influence—intact and without catching a bullet—was an art form that Dante clearly mastered. As for retribution, anyone who gave him trouble was bought off, scared off, or broken.

I should know.

Dante had four weaknesses, in the form of his lovely daughters.

His second-youngest died from a heroin overdose—even though she never used the stuff. The eldest daughter was driven off a very high overpass and died on the way to the hospital. Dante's youngest kid dove between him and an assassin's bullet. That same shot not only killed her but left Dante confined to a wheelchair, minus some of his spine.

Rather than get surgery, cybernetics, or even a new body, the infamous mastermind retired from the game. Word spread, of course. Within six months, rumors abounded that Dante was reduced to a devastated recluse on an uncharted island. But which one? Even his lieutenants didn't know.

Then again, Dante's woes were a bit more complicated. The press thought his daughters' deaths were unrelated. I knew otherwise because I killed them—and left Dante in that fancy wheelchair of his.

Each hit involved weeks of planning and surveillance. I covered my tracks so well that even Interpol thought my first two kills were accidents. Everyone was fooled, except for Dante. The old man was behind more than his fair share of "untraceable" kills. He brought his surviving child here for her protection (and his).

Naturally, the pudgy Chilean wanted vengeance. With as many enemies as Dante had, I doubted he would find us first. My cruel actions were initially spawned by revenge. Yet, the more I studied Dante, the more my motives shifted toward greed . . . and beyond.

With the old man's resources, I could probably invade five small countries—at once—and win. Dante's accumulated wealth acquired interest within thousands of well-disguised accounts. This didn't include the daily inflow of cash from his various criminal enterprises.

By my estimates, the old man had $588.1 billion in the coffers. Split three ways, that was a lot of goddamned money. Even with the old man in seclusion, his top lieutenants remained "loyal." Eventually, one or more of the power-hungry bastards would've pulled a coup.

That's why we hit Dante first.

Keegly used his weather powers to pummel the island with multiple tornados. Most of Dante's people were caught out in the open, during a beautiful spring afternoon. Once the drone defenses were neutralized, Raimy went in.

The one-man army chuted in with enough weapons and tech to kill dozens—then duplicated himself a few hundred times over. The more psychic clones Raimy created, the shorter their life spans. I figured this many would last about an hour, which was more than enough time.

Most of Dante's people were human. Any supers who survived the tornados and Raimy's psychic clones were my problem. Dante was personally protected by five supers, who warranted my attention. I killed them without a fuss, then shot their boss. Riddled with bullets, Dante even recognized me, just before I parked the last two rounds in his face.

We hit them so fast and hard that they only managed to delete eighteen percent of their mainframe files. The information we recovered gave us plenty of insights into their criminal network. The blackmail alone was fucking priceless.

Then there was Dante's cowering money launderer. We timed our strike to catch him on the island. The poor bastard wet his pants when my gunshots splattered some of Dante's blood across his face. Before I could even ask for the account data, the investment geek unscrewed his left pinkie-slash-flash-drive.

Every last account was on the gadget. I oversaw the ransacking of poor Dante's liquid assets, which were transferred to our hidden accounts. Best of all, my math was way off. The old man was worth $1.51 trillion.

Our funds were equally and fairly split. Raimy's clones gave each other high fives, then shot the accountant. I circled the island a few times and killed a few dozen more minions. Then I found Dante's private microbrewery.

That's how I ended up here, with the gold cooler full of beers (and one of Dante's cigars in my mouth). Behind me were raging storm clouds, complete with bolts of lightning that stabbed down at unnatural intervals. Keegly must've been sorting out the stragglers. The tropical beach was covered in examples of his handiwork: from building debris to bodies (including my "human pillow").

Once I tied off the last details, I'd call down the *North Wind* and slip into the night. Our foul-mouthed dropship carried three tactical nukes, two of which would be dumped on this island to cover our tracks. After all, once Dante's people realized their boss was dead, they'd go on the warpath—

"Found her!" yelled Raimy (or one of his clones).

The hawk-faced killer wore dark-green ceramic body armor, tac fatigues, and most of his arsenal. Any minute now, they should start blinking out of existence. Five of them marched Isabella de la Dante toward me with her hands tied behind her back. Her boobs were fake, but her voluptuous curves weren't. Thanks to her late father's taste in mistresses, neither was her face.

Dressed in a crimson one-piece swimsuit, Dante's surviving daughter was covered in grime and dried blood. Her long black hair was a wet mess as she struggled against her captors and cursed us in Spanish. While he sought out his daughters' killer, the old man groomed Isabella to take over his empire.

Dante's two oldest daughters cashed out their trust funds, disowned their father, and pursued honest lives. The youngest (who took a bullet for him) was his favorite of the four and likely successor. Isabella was a high-ranking advisor with no apparent interest in running the family cartel.

Then I came along and made her Dante's only choice. Already well-versed in the business, Isabella stepped up beyond even her father's expectations. Given the chance, she might've done him proud.

Alas, we'll never know. For our plans to work, Isabella had to die, along with everyone else on this island.

"Thought you might wanna do the honors," one of the Raimys offered with a dirty wink.

I rolled my eyes. The duplicator had a weakness for women of color, even during high-risk ops. Gangbanging the Latina, with his own clones, was Raimy's idea of fun.

Me?

I preferred drunken one-nighters with sluts who didn't cuddle.

"Knock yourselves out, Raimy," I muttered with a dismissive frown. "Just be quick. We're gone in twenty."

One of his clones unexpectedly blinked away— which only happened when his power was tapped out.

"More than enough time," Raimy replied.

The remaining clones picked Isabella up and carried her (kicking and screaming) toward the jungle. Raimy grabbed a bottle, clinked his to mine, then rushed off with his pals. The sun continued to set. Just before I finished my beer, the storms on the other side of the island abruptly ceased.

A few minutes later, Keegly soared into view. Unlike Raimy or myself, the aging weather wielder didn't like tactical attire, guns, or explosives. The tanned pothead favored a pair of leather sandals, a tie-dyed bowling shirt, and old jeans. About the only gadget he carried was a modified smartphone (one that his powers wouldn't easily fry). A residual storm breeze played around with his thick gray locks.

"We done here?" Keegly wearily asked as he neatly landed beside me.

With a nod and a smile, I reached into the cooler and tossed him a brew.

"How much?" he asked.

"$1.51 *trillion*, old friend."

"Damn!" Keegly reacted with quiet amazement, while I grabbed another beer for myself. "Our figures were way the hell off. You think all that money's his?"

I thoughtfully popped the cap.

"Good question," I shrugged. "What're you gonna do with your cut?"

"I'm going to save the environment," Keegly replied, "while screwing every young hippie girl I can find."

"Sounds righteous," I replied before I clinked my bottle to his.

"What about you, kid?" he asked.

"I'm gonna find some talent and hit the next mark," I replied.

Keegly half-choked on his beer, then blocked my sun.

"You settled the score, Alex. *You've won*," he preached. "Walk away and find some happiness while your luck's good and your enemies haven't piled up—like Dante's."

I thought of Samantha and the kids. Of how Dante's people killed them . . .

"Can't," I shrugged.

Almost three years ago, Dante sent killers into my home. I was away while my family was viciously murdered. They died because I couldn't be bought off. Sadly, my superiors weren't as incorruptible. That's why I turned in my badge.

After the funeral, Keegly and Raimy offered to help settle the score. Keegly taught me everything I knew about being a super cop. Raimy and I met at Quantico and went through so many doors together.

Turning them into executioners wasn't my intent.

As we tore through Dante's cartel, one sad thing became clear. There were so many "untouchable" villains out there. Well-dressed fiends who managed to buy their freedom with blood money. These bastards didn't deserve justice.

They deserved me.

Isabella's screams cut through the air, mixed by whoops of joy from Raimy and his clones. Keegly gave me a knowing frown.

"We're gonna sit back and let this happen?" he frowned with distaste.

"Having morals didn't save my family," I told him. "Why have 'em now?"

The weather wielder regarded me with open contempt.

"What's happened to you, kid?" Keegly asked.

"To my soul, you mean?" I asked with a grin. "Check the trash. Maybe you'll find it there."

He started to reply when a sniper round exited the jungle. It came from either Raimy's rifle or one of his clones'. I was fast enough to react. The air even crystallized around me whenever I moved hyper-fast, like a temporary layer of armor.

I could've caught the armor-piercing round before it hit poor Keegly's skull. Instead, I sat on my ass while the shot went through his mouth mid-word. The timing wasn't perfect, as the round shattered his two front teeth. Keegly's eyes went wide as the bullet punched through the back of his skull. Brains and bone splattered to the sand . . . followed by the tumbling corpse.

Sorry, old friend.

I turned as Isabella emerged from the tree line. Covered in Raimys' blood (or his clones'), the curvy Latina was now seven feet tall and rippled with a muscled, bulletproof physique. Her swimsuit was specially made to adjust whenever she kicked on her power. As she towered over me, Isabella made Raimy's rifle look like a children's toy.

"Problems?" I asked.

Isabella shook her head as her body crackled for a moment. Then she quick-shrank back to her normal size. The ability to alter one's physique was rarely acquired through birth.

Like her boobs, the enhancement was bought and paid for by her late father. Dante must've figured that making her able to throw tanks around would keep her safe.

If he only knew . . .

After our first few hits on Dante's operations, Isabella tracked us down and caught me alone. Instead of having me killed, she made one helluva juicy offer. I'd kill her sisters and father—based on her intel.

Once my partners were dead, we'd split the cash two ways. Isabella would take over her daddy's organization and I'd have my revenge. We'd ignore each other and that would be that.

Isabella sealed the deal with some sweaty sex, then left a target package for her siblings. Within a month, they were dead. While her daddy sought answers—and revenge—Isabella gave me the intel necessary for today's raid.

What surprised me was that she didn't lead us into a trap. After all, Isabella was already Dante's sole heir. All the paperwork was locked in. His lieutenants knew it too.

All she had to do was have us killed and wait. Sooner or later, Dante would've handed her the keys to a massive empire. Lucky me.

"That was fun," Isabella grinned with a slight Chilean accent. "When does our ride get here?"

I frowned down at my watch, then tossed her the last beer in the cooler.

"Fifteen minutes," I replied.

Isabella popped the cap and thirstily consumed a quarter of it. Then she eyed Keegly's corpse.

"I understand you wanting Raimy dead," she said with a disgusted glance toward the treeline. "Why Keegly? I thought you adored him."

I finished off my beer and tossed the bottle away.

"He was my conscience—something I'll never need again," I muttered before I stood up, walked over, and kissed Isabella's blood-soaked lips. Then I took her bottle.

"Grab a quick swim," I urged with a casual smile as I sipped her beer. "You're a bloody mess."

Isabella studied me for a moment, then shook her head with a knowing grin. Having grown up with killers, she wasn't surprised (or appalled) by my actions. I figured she'd try to kill me on the way back to the mainland—once she secured the assets, of course.

If Dante's lieutenants ever learned of her betrayal, Isabella wouldn't last a week. Nor would they follow her if she didn't avenge her old man. Her looming double-cross was the third reason I gave her a poisoned beer. The second was that I was starting to like her. And the main reason I killed Isabella de la Dante was that she meant to salvage her father's cartel.

Fuck that.

As I watched that fine ass disappear into the calm surf, I sipped more of the poisoned beer. Like all of the others, I laced them with something quick and painless. It was my little failsafe, in case one of them didn't die so easy. The toxin wasn't cheap. Neither was the antidote that coursed through my veins.

THE BRIGAND

Within the darkened living room, Eric Tooles heard the spacious apartment's front door unlock. The patient killer took up a position at the end of the hallway and around the corner. In his gloved hands was a suppressor-capped Glock 17.

Feeling under-equipped, the assassin only sported street attire tonight. Work boots, black jeans, a dark gray t-shirt, and a gray sports jacket. The clothes were purchased secondhand and would be torched when the job was done.

The target, Carmen Munroe, was a writer who specialized in modern-day occultism. She had something of an underground following, which would've been fine: *if magic wasn't real.* Super powers, cybernetics, and the presence of aliens were proven quantities.

Magic was trickier because most people's minds lacked the capacity to believe in it. That's why it was commonly viewed as myth and folklore. Most humans could only accept the existence of magic after a firsthand experience.

Tooles and his younger brother, Saul, used to break into houses for a living. One wintry night, they broke into a vampire's house. Things went bad and the house went up in flames.

Saul made it out—until his older brother hunted him down and put a wooden stake through his heart. After that gruesome experience, Tooles became a professional taker of lives, who only killed mystics or those who did business with them. He killed for money, favors, and whenever the mood struck him.

While Munroe knew plenty of truths about the mystical world, she hadn't caught on to the need for discretion. Her books gave away more secrets than mankind needed to know. That's why an anonymous client paid him six figures to shut her up. After the author was disposed of, other parties would do the same with her published works. Within three years, Carmen Munroe would fade into obscurity, as would the potential threat she posed.

A normal person typically stumbled across magic in one of two ways. Sometimes, a person was entrusted with the knowledge and sworn to secrecy. Or, that person was lucky enough to survive a mystical experience. Those few who pulled through often kept the secret—so as to avoid any quality time in a psych ward.

But every so often, there was someone with an obsessive need to spread the hidden truths of magic across the modern world. These enlightened fools were killed for the greater good. The general public didn't need to know that magic existed . . . or what dangers it posed.

Some of Munroe's sources were mystics, who shared the author's misguided mindset. They griped that magic should be "outed" to the public. In their minds, magic could save the world where technology couldn't.

On the surface, it was an appealing argument.

The right rituals could turn deserts into forests within a matter of days. Diseases could be cured via alchemy. Murdered innocents could be resurrected.

The possibilities were many . . . but so was the cost.

That much power wasn't easy to find. Those who had it never gave it away (without strings). Then there was the ultimate flaw—human nature. With the right relics, a single ambitious soul could control the world or burn it to a cinder. Cynics, like Tooles, understood this harsh reality all too well. He also agreed with his client's assessment that logic wouldn't work on Munroe—nor would threats.

Motion lighting kicked on. A woman's high heels clacked down the hallway's hardwood floor.

Tooles' instructions were to make Carmen Munroe dead and dispose of the body. Her files and backups were all located and accounted for. He'd swept her place for artifacts (twice) and found none.

All he had to do was whip around the corner and fire. Once the deed was done, the killer meant to use his assassin's ring. The white ivory artifact was given to him as payment for a past job. With it, Tooles could turn Munroe's corpse into salt (down to her blood and clothing). Then he'd pour her remains down a toilet and flush.

Most of his targets didn't rate such extensive disposal. He made an exception because some of the author's occult associates might try to avenge her death. If he left a body for them to find, they could use it (and magic) to track him down.

It was seventeen paces from the front door to his corner. As Munroe approached, he waited for the tenth step. Then Tooles swung around the corner, lined up on her forehead . . . and held his fire with a worried frown.

In her late thirties, the round-faced author's stylish red dress hugged her plumpish curves and showed a firm pair of legs. The milky skinned target wore curly brown locks halfway down her back.

Why didn't he put two rounds through her head?

Carmen Munroe *appeared to be sleepwalking.* The author's eyeballs danced around beneath her eyelids. That condition wasn't in her file, which meant (in all likelihood) that she was something's puppet. Then he noticed something else: a men's copper bracelet around her right wrist.

Covered with battle glyphs, it looked very old. The killer kept the Glock trained on his victim, who playfully raised her hands.

"Aren't you going to shoot me?" she asked with a male voice and a mild French accent.

"Shit!" Tooles muttered as a hulking metal form abruptly took her place. He couldn't tell if she was in the armor or if Munroe *turned into the armor itself.* He'd seen both enchantments before.

At six-five, the stylishly imposing armor was a mix of silvery plate and chainmail. A visored mask completely covered the face and eyes. A red chainmail hood fit loosely over the black helm. When both fists clenched, the black-and-red gauntlets made a grinding sound.

Tooles stepped back and holstered the useless Glock. Armor this well-made could probably ignore anything short of an anti-tank weapon.

"I heard you were fearless, Mr. Tooles," taunted the armor. "That's why I arranged your hire."

The ruthless killer pursed his bearded lips for a confused moment.

"You want me to kill your host?" asked Tooles.

"Exactly," it replied.

"Why?" asked the assassin.

"So I can bond with *you.*"

"Come again?" Tooles balked as he took another step back.

"Let me explain," gestured the armor with its massive gauntlets. "I was crafted during the Crusades to protect some French prick, whose name I can't even remember. Then I became a family heirloom until one of his descendants lost me in a poker game in '72. Since then, I've been passed around like a poorly valued antiquity."

Without a host (and the right conditions), a sentient artifact couldn't trigger. Instead, it would collect dust. More than a few of them even went mad from neglect.

Tooles understood that. What he didn't know was what triggered the bracelet. It could've been a mystical phrase, imminent danger, or any number of other factors. Or, perhaps, the enchantment's safeguards had eroded, to the point where the artifact could seize control of a sleeping host.

"Then Carmen found me," sighed the artifact. "The bitch had such potential."

Intrigued, Tooles folded his arms. "What went wrong?"

"I shared my knowledge of the occult, figuring that she would use me to build an empire," seethed the armor. "What did Carmen do with this priceless gift? She wrangled a fucking book deal!"

"And if you walked her into traffic, you might've ended up on a shelf for decades," Tooles reasoned.

"I belong on the battlefield," argued the armor. "End this cow, then bond with me, Mr. Tooles. *I'll make you legendary.*"

Tooles thoughtfully rocked back and forth on booted feet.

"What makes me so special?" asked the assassin. "Why not bond with a wizard or a demigod? I'm just a worker bee with a gun."

"Don't be so modest, Mr. Tooles," replied the armor. "You're a self-taught killer, with a known taste for killing mystics. More importantly, you've managed to avoid being owned by any of the varied factions of this world."

Tooles frowned at how well this artifact knew him.

"What a pair we'd make, huh?" he stalled.

"Exactly," replied the armor. "End this bitch and I'll lay the world at your feet. What say you?"

"Um, what do I call you?" Tooles asked as he made up his mind.

"I've gone by many names," replied the armor. "Since you're a thief-turned-killer, call me '*Brigand.*'"

"I like that," Tooles agreed through an approving chuckle. "Now, if you'd kindly pop the hood, I'll kill your host."

"Finally!" Brigand sighed as it raised the visor. "Set me free of this one."

In spite of the armor's massive size, the sleeping face of Carmen Munroe was underneath. Tooles studied his victim's relatively small face for a moment, then drew his Glock. He racked the slide and approached the helpless host.

"Fire away, Mr. Tooles," the armor purred through her lips.

Tooles shifted the pistol to his left hand, then broke the author's nose with a fast right jab. Both Munroe and Brigand screamed in unison as the armor flowed into the bracelet like inhaled air. Fully awake and agonized, Carmen Munroe dropped to her knees.

The killer seized the back of the author's head with his right hand, then jammed the Glock's suppressor against her windpipe. The author looked up at him through tearing brown eyes.

"Remove the bracelet," Tooles sternly ordered. "I'll give you 'til the count of three—"

Before he could reach one, Munroe pulled the bracelet off and tossed it away.

"Just take it and go!" she pleaded. "You don't have to kill me!"

Tooles pondered his situation.

The killer's ethics required him to see the job through. Half of the fee was in his account. Still, since the job was a trap, he didn't expect to see the rest of it.

"Ms. Munroe, what happens if you tell a soul about tonight?" Tooles asked.

Munroe licked her quivering lips. "You'll track me down and kill me?"

"Along with your chatty mystic pals," vowed the killer. "Now, give me your left shoe."

She frowned at the odd command, took it off, and handed it over. With a curt nod, Tooles backed away toward the artifact. Too terrified to move, Munroe watched him use her shoe to scoop up the bracelet. Not in the mood to even touch the artifact, Tooles knew that a smelly shoe would have to suffice.

"Sorry about the nose," Tooles shrugged as he headed for the door.

"T-thank you," Munroe smiled, finally free to help bring about the mystical salvation of this world—

Until Tooles turned and put two silenced rounds through her chest. Why'd he change his mind, just then? Because the Brigand did pay him half. Even with this setup, Tooles had his reputation to consider.

The killer holstered his gun and considered his assassin's ring. With a sigh, he tapped the author's wide-eyed corpse and turned it into a salt outline. He wouldn't flush it. The "signature" kill might convince her friends to adhere to the mystical norms of secrecy—or else.

Whether they sought revenge or not, he'd be ready.

As for the Brigand, Tooles meant to call in some favors and have its enchantments looked over. If they could be fixed, the killer would have it done—then sell it to a reasonable buyer. If the belligerent artifact was simply too far gone, Tooles wouldn't have it destroyed.

He'd save it for a rainy day . . .

THE DEVIOUS CAPTAIN

The third moon just started to rise when Ayrim Wanderfoot reached the inn. The only reasons to come through this muddy village were to trade livestock, risk disease at the local brothel, or drink at the Bearded Elk. Having waited here three nights, I spent most of my time at the brothel or the inn.

Mine was a simple errand. Now that Ayrim finally arrived, I could deliver my message and ride home. With luck, my former captain would come with me. He approached the inn's hitching post and wearily dismounted. I approached on foot, with my arms outstretched in the universal language of parlay.

The hooded rider spotted me immediately. Ayrim's gloved hands drifted toward his sword, until he recognized me. *He'd better!* I saved his neck at the Siege of Peltor. Granted, I would've done the same for any of my countrymen. Still, the once-famed captain's life was worth far more than an average soldier of the crown's (even mine).

The lad was a masterful archer, a devious tactician, and the youngest captain to ever rank in any army. With enough details and a bit of time to dwell on them, AyrimWanderfoot could outwit a roomful of generals. That's what King Sorim needed right now: someone who could unite the Middle Realms and win the war to come.

Ayrim took a cautious glance over his right and left shoulders, then approached me with a wary smile.

"Ufil, Son of Vim!" he greeted with an extended hand. "What are you doing this far south?"

I clasped his hand and brought him in for a grinning hug.

"Looking for you, lad," I replied, then stepped back. Under the light of a large lantern, I saw a hardened ex-soldier who lost his innocence and hopes to my foolhardy king. At eight-and-twenty years, his bearded menace and scholar's eyes were a fitting blend. Ayrim looked well enough. Beneath the brown riding cloak was the light gray armor of a mercenary. He had six throwing knives (that I could see) sheathed across his person, with a small shield on his mare's left side. Slung across his back was a bow made from pure elvensteel—a gift he earned for averting an unnecessary war. His quiver was half-empty, which implied a busy day on the road.

After he left the king's service, I heard tales of Ayrim's exploits with that bow. He went from fighting wars to settling grudges. While his clients were mostly noble, his methods were quite the opposite. Whenever possible, Ayrim preferred to kill the wealthy—whether they deserved to die or not. He also went after bandits, wild creatures, and even the occasional demon.

Ayrim didn't work for coin because his targets were often well-pursed. The former captain took these quests to stay sharp and acquire favors. That's how I tracked him down: by the multitude of grateful folk who owed Ayrim for past services.

He led me into the Bearded Elk, asked for two cups and a bottle of the good stuff. When Ayrim paid in silver, the bartender reluctantly parted with a large, unmarked bottle. My former captain headed for a corner table that was currently occupied by four large swords-for-hire.

Probably there to protect a caravan of livestock, they looked up as Ayrim approached. Without hesitation, they nervously grabbed their drinks and fled the table.

"Friends of yours?" I chuckled.

"We have an understanding," Ayrim replied before he set the cups and bottle down. "What's it been? Eight winters?"

"Seven," I replied.

Ayrim unslung his bow and set it beside him. Then he drew the sword and sat down. I frowned as he placed the blade across his lap.

"Expecting trouble?" I asked.

"Not until I saw you, old friend," Ayrim replied.

I took an empty chair and sat across from him. With my back to the door, anyone coming in would have to shoot around me to get to him.

"Tell me that you don't still serve that venereal worm," groaned Ayrim.

"We need you," I manfully begged. "The Relterru are finally preparing to march."

With piqued interest, Ayrim removed the cork with his teeth, then poured some mead into my cup.

"When will they reach the Middle Realm?" he asked.

"By the heart of winter, according to the king's spies," I replied.

Ayrim's eyes narrowed and for good reason. It was almost summer. The Relterru were at their military peak and wouldn't need so long to prepare for an invasion. So why wait?

The king's advisors were divided over the enemy's strategy. Some argued that their "winter invasion" was a ruse of some kind. Others feared that their mages would (somehow) transport their army over, under, or through an unguarded peak of the Talon Massif—the natural barrier between us and the Northern Realms.

Ayrim thoughtfully leaned back into his chair. Despite myself, I tried to guess what he'd say next.

"Have you seen any movement along the sea?" he asked.

"No," I frowned. "Besides, a fleet of thousands could be destroyed by a well-placed storm spell. They'll move through the Talon."

"Then why would they attack us in winter?" Ayrim asked with an intrigued smile.

"Enlighten this tired old man," I sighed.

Instead of a timely reply, Ayrim raised his cup. With a patient smile, I did the same.

"To lost friends, buxom maidens, and dead foes," he toasted. We clanked cups and drank.

"Mmm!" I purred. "That's not the usual swill."

"What's the point of earning coin if you can't drink the good stuff?" Ayrim said, just before he realized something. Whatever it was put a conniving grin on his face.

"Answer my question," I insisted.

"Being northerners, the Relterru fight well in the snow," he explained. "More importantly, *you don't*. The Middle Realms haven't had a winter war in centuries. The Relterru will wait for the harvest, poison or burn the food stores, then sow chaos. When the snows fall, expect them to plow through the Middle Realms with a set plan and reckless haste. If you try to outmaneuver them, you'll lose men and resources along the way. If I'm right, those who can't hide behind warm walls will die from the sword, hunger, or cold."

It was a delight to watch his mind work—even when he described an unbeatable foe. The Relterru had just slaughtered the last rival kingdom north of the Talon. Their simple aim was to head south and destroy the rest of the realms. Without a foe to conquer and destroy, their varied houses would've killed themselves off by now.

It wasn't about land or wealth. All that mattered was how much blood they could spill. Every Relterru—down to their children—had a warrior's temper. Some say it was a curse from the gods. A few scholars called it a trait within their blood, through which they've survived the harsher northern climes. Wherever it came from, the Relterru were only united when at war.

There were only four castes within their society. Their leaders schemed and fought. Their warriors fought. Their mystics fought. And their slaves suffered.

Worried for my family, I grabbed the bottle and poured myself half a cup.

"How will their first strike come?" I asked.

"They're already here," Ayrim declared with a confident smile. "A hundred-strong, at least. I'd send battle mages instead of mere saboteurs."

I groaned at the idea.

Battle mages were powerful, dangerous, and hard to replace. It took decades to learn war magicks and the Relterru had the very best. We had more mages but that wasn't the point. If a hundred of them infiltrated the Middle Realms . . .

"I'd dress them as civilians and smuggle them on merchant ships," shrugged Ayrim. "They'll destroy the food stores, assassinate key targets, and hinder your mobilizations in every possible way."

"Then what?" I asked.

Ayrim chuckled. "When the snows fall, I'd expect a full strike against the Eastern Pass."

"The garrison there's strong enough to hold them," I reminded him. "Also, Tolden's less than a day's ride."

Ayrim drained his cup with a contented sigh.

"It's the easiest way to win," argued my former captain. "All three garrisons draw supplies and men from Tolden. The Eastern Pass is closest. Smash the garrison, take the city, and they'll have a foothold on our side of the Talon. Your nearest reinforcements are what? Four days away?"

It bothered me that his plan made sense.

"By the time a sizeable army caught up to them, the Relterru could burn their way to the Lesser Sea," he estimated. "Now, what does your rat nipple of a king want me to do about it?"

"King Sorim's amassing an army," I explained. "All of the Middle Realms will participate. He wants you to help lead it."

My mention of "help" made Ayrim smile as I slid him the bottle. He refilled the cup and looked past me.

"In other words, I do the fighting and Sorim gets the glory?"

"The king's offering you two chests of gold, a royal pardon, lands, and title," I offered. "Also, if you do this, I'll consider us even."

With a laughing shake of the head, Ayrim downed his cup, stood up, and stretched. The room went quiet as all eyes rested upon his gripped sword.

"Sorry, old friend, but I'm desperate," I pleaded. "If we can take them on, we'd have them outnumbered four-to-one—"

"Did Peltor teach you nothing?" Ayrim snapped. "The barbarians had us outnumbered eight-to-one, and *we slaughtered them*. Why?"

"Because we had Peltor's rickety walls to protect us, along with the high ground," I conceded.

"The Relterru won't fight us on open ground until it suits them," Ayrim assured me. "Expect night attacks, plague magic, assassinations, and every other honorless trick imaginable. When they're ready, they'll destroy Sorim's 'grand army' in one battle. Then you'll be defenseless."

"What should we do?" I asked.

Ayrim looked down at his sword, then sat back down. He didn't sheath the blade or slip it on his lap. Deep in thought, he held it point-down like a walking cane.

"Forgive me, Ufil," Ayrim apologized. "I will never serve that coward again. Send your family south and I'll see to their care."

"If the Relterru get past the Talon Massif, then no place is safe," I pleaded. "Give me a way to save our people. *Please!*"

"They're not my people anymore," Ayrim replied with a bitter scowl. "Ride home and get your family to safety, Ufil. Then tell that whore of a king to collapse all three passes, empty Tolden, then raze the city."

"The king won't destroy our oldest citadel," I reminded him.

"If he can't keep it, why let it stand?" Ayrim bitterly countered. "Once you explain that to the fool, he'll need to persuade the other kings to keep their armies at home and at the ready."

"Ahh," I nodded. "So when one kingdom's attacked, the other armies can cut off the Relterru from different directions?"

"Something like that," Ayrim nodded with a determined look on his face. It was the same look he had when he learned of King Sorim's plan to expel the elven merchants from his land—and steal whatever they left behind. Against orders, the captain personally escorted hundreds of elven families (and their wealth) through hostile lands and to the safety of their forests.

In return, the hero was branded a traitor and banished by his king, on pain of death.

"Where will you be?" I asked.

Ayrim sheathed his sword and picked up the bow.

"Killing Relterru spies," he muttered. "If I learn anything interesting, I'll send word."

"What if they're all battle mages?" I asked.

Ayrim flicked his bowstring and fiery white glyphs appeared along its surface—all etched in elvish. After a few seconds, the glyphs faded away into the dulled metal surface.

"Then I'll get to spend their coin," winked the grizzled merc. "Either way, Ufil, this makes us even."

THE DIVA

This was a score to brag about (not that any of us ever could).

It was simple and virtually gun-free. Instead of the usual high-speed getaway driving, all I had to do was arrange transportation for a kidnapping. That's why I was behind the wheel of a stolen plumbing van, with *the* Damea Gency in the back.

The twenty-three-year-old pop star/actress/hostage was finer than Angelina Jolie in her prime. I could practically smell her money—

"Slow it down!" Curtis yelled through the partition.

I glanced down at the speedometer and saw I was doing eighty on a two-lane California road. Curtis was right (like always). This was speed trap heaven. The last thing we needed was to get pulled over by some bored deputy.

I got my head back into the crime, slowed down, and eyed the driver's side mirror. Nobody was near us. A few miles later, we passed a welcome sign to the great state of Nevada. A full moon lit up the flat, arid landscape like some kind of high-powered stellar flashlight.

Another hour later, we arrived at the safe house; an old, single-story ranch home with peeling white paint and a huge front lawn. A hundred feet behind the house was an old wooden barn in desperate need of a paint job. Rusty farm equipment and overgrown grass took up the rest of the place, which had definitely seen better days.

It was the last place anyone would look for us. Curtis had picked the spot last month, while Lara and Eddie set up surveillance. Joe and Vera Wrenlip owned the property, lived alone, and didn't get out much. On weekends, they shopped, went to the movies, and spent time at a local Methodist church. During the week, Vera painted landscapes while Joe spent most of his waking hours watching cable and making model planes.

Neither of them had a steady social media presence or spent much time on the phone. None of their family was nearby or kept in frequent contact. The closest neighbor was over a mile away. Their only regular visitor was the mailman, which meant that there shouldn't be any unwanted guests for the next couple of days.

That should be more than enough time.

So, while Curtis and I kidnapped the "2020 Sexiest Woman Alive," Eddie and Lara paid the Wrenlips a visit with a twelve-gauge shotgun. Hopefully, the couple didn't give Eddie any lip. The first-generation illegal alien (and Chi town thug) had too much body art to go with his short temper.

At least he was a solid entry man. Eddie also didn't know when to be afraid. If the shit came down, he'd throw fists or lead. With this much money at stake, Curtis figured that we'd need him to case the house and handle security. Still, Eddie sometimes killed people when they upset him—which was why Lara tagged along.

Curtis' fiancée was a self-taught money launderer with a Computer Science degree from MIT. Blessed with decent looks and an honest face, she was almost as good with people as Curtis. With her at the scene, Eddie would probably behave. Even he wasn't stupid enough to wreck this score.

I parked the van in the barn, right next to the getaway cars. While the red Toyota Celica and the white Saturn sedan looked like rusted, beat-up clunkers, they weren't where it counted. I tweaked them both to the point where they'd outrun any cop car on the road.

I killed the van's engine, stepped out into the arid night, and went over the last leg of the plan. All we had to do was wait for Damea to wake up. Eddie would scare the accounts and passwords out of her, then Curtis would dose her again.

Once the money was stolen, we'd torch the van, the barn, and the house—to remove any useful evidence. We'd leave the Wrenlips safely bound and gagged outside, then call 9-1-1 (on their behalf) when we were safely away. Then we'd drive right back to California, dump the starlet in a pre-paid motel room, and part ways.

I pulled a black ski mask out of my pocket and put it on. It didn't clash with my blue plumber coveralls and black driving gloves. Our street clothes were packed in the cars and would stay there until we left.

The back of the van opened and out stepped Curtis. During the drive, Curtis changed out of his fancy black suit and into a set of plumber coveralls, a blue ski mask, and white surgical gloves. In his mid-forties and built like a mid-sized quarterback, our fearless leader could charm a lesbian straight. The brains behind this caper, my fellow ex-con could've hustled an honest fortune when he left the joint. But, like me, Curtis hated honest work.

He carefully picked up Damea Gency and carried her from the van. The drugged Grammy winner wore a revealing black party dress. Her shoes were off, and her toenails were painted blue. Her tanned, five-six frame was nothing shy of athletic, C-cupped perfection.

A black hood covered her gorgeous face and most of her long black hair. When Curtis placed her in my arms, I was too shocked to move. He flashed me a knowing smile through the ski mask.

"Not every day you have a diva in your arms, is it?" he asked.

"Got that right," I whispered.

"Get her inside," Curtis ordered.

Eddie opened the door as I reached the porch. At thirty-one, he wore the same brand of blue coveralls that Curtis and I wore, along with a black ski mask and blue surgical gloves. A sawed-off single-barrel pump was casually slung over his left shoulder.

Back in our days at Joliet, Eddie and Curtis liked to hit the free weights while I preferred basketball. Once we got out, Curtis let himself go a bit—but not Eddie. He wanted to show off his perfect pecs and thick arms until the day he died. Seeing as he was short and ugly, he figured the ladies deserved a distraction.

"C'mon! C'mon!" Eddie whispered, his Mexican accent full of tension.

I carefully carried Damea through the living room. The air conditioner was set to maximum, which put a smile on my face. Then a quick pang of guilt hit me when I noticed the dozen-plus photos of kids and grandkids all along the Wrenlips' walls. This time tomorrow, they'd be a pile of ashes—along with the rest of the house.

Curtis caught up to us on the way to the dining room. The furniture was cleared away, with only dirty beige carpeting to offend the eye. In their place was a rolling stool and portable computer station. A laptop, wires, and other "tech stuff" were stacked on a three-tiered rolling cart.

Curtis tapped me on the back and gestured toward a far wall. I gently sat Damea down so that she leaned against the corner. Eddie quickly tied her ankles and hands together with white rope.

"Any problems with the Wrenlips?" Curtis asked.

"Not a one," Eddie replied, half-distracted by Damea's low-cut bustline. "I gave 'em both a shot at sundown."

Curtis checked his watch with an approving smile, then looked up when Lara stepped out of the bathroom. Dressed like us, her surgical gloves were purple (to match her ski mask). Short and nervous, she stood up on her toes and gave Curtis a quick kiss.

In her early twenties, Lara had never pulled a "hands-on" felony before. Luckily, her first real score would be enough to retire on.

"Do we really have to wear all of this crap?" Lara asked.

"Yeah," Curtis replied as he sized up our hostage. "That gal's got a serious resistance to roofies. There's no telling when she'll wake up."

"As long as she forgets tonight—and your face," Lara frowned.

"After the stuff I used, she'll wonder what day it is," Curtis assured her.

"How many did you slip her?" I asked.

"I put one in her wine glass at the party, which should've been enough to drop someone twice her size," Curtis said. "When that didn't work, I talked her into a moonlit walk and gave her a shot when she wasn't looking."

"Real smooth," Lara commented with a hint of jealousy. "Can't wait to hear how you did that."

Curtis gave her a reassuring grin.

"What if she's a closet junkie?" Eddie asked. "She might O.D. on us."

"She'd have done it by now," Curtis countered. "Either way, I brought a kit along. If push comes to shove—"

Damea slowly began to stir.

"What the hell?" Curtis frowned as he glanced at his watch. "How is she awake?"

"Doesn't matter," Lara said with a nod to Eddie, who handed her the twelve-gauge. "Let's get this over with."

The Mexican knelt by Damea, who woke up with a dazed moan. Clumsily, she tried to stand, only to realize that her hands and feet were bound. When she tried to pull her hood off, Eddie grinned and playfully pulled her hands away from it.

"Wha-? What's going on?" Damea asked.

"Ms. Gency, I'm afraid you've been kidnapped," Eddie revealed with practiced menace.

Our hostage was silent for a few moments. . . then she began to laugh. Even quarter-stoned, her voice was beautiful.

"April Fool's Day was last week, guys!" Damea giggled.

With his right hand, Eddie pulled his small black pocketknife and flicked out a serrated blade. Then he yanked off her hood with his free hand. Damea's mesmerizing green eyes blinked under the harsh dining room lighting.

Her smile died at the sight of Eddie's four-inch blade. He held the tip right in front of her left eye with the stillness of a surgeon. Through the ski mask, Eddie gave her his patented "street" glare. Damea cringed and backed against the wall with real fright in her eyes . . .

Good.

"Sorry to borrow you, Ms. Gency," Eddie said with a grin. "But you have something we want."

"W-what?" Damea gasped as she looked up at each of us. "What do you want?!"

"The password to your offshore accounts," Eddie continued. "The ones worth forty million Euros."

"So, this is a real kidnapping?" Damea asked.

"Yes!" Eddie replied with growing impatience.

"I'm not on some hidden camera show or something?"

"Does this feel fake to you?" Eddie asked as he gently pressed the tip of the knife against her throat.

That's when Damea Gency made her move. The rope on her wrists snapped as her dainty hands wrapped around Eddie's thick right wrist and twisted. Bones broke and the knife fell—just before she shoved Eddie at the ceiling!

The poor bastard screamed like a child during his short, painful flight. Then his back hit the ceiling hard enough to leave a crack. Eddie fell, hit the carpet face-first, and stopped moving.

The diva easily snapped the rope around her ankles and jumped up with an eager smile. Lara started to level the shotgun at our "helpless" hostage but Damea was too fast. The diva snapped the weapon across the middle with a left-handed chop.

Lara stepped back in shock and dropped her now-useless shotgun. That's when Curtis blindsided Damea with an overhand left to the temple. She should've dropped. I'd seen him do it a dozen times over the years and it never failed (until now).

The diva's bare right heel kick connected with Curtis' chest. He went flying hard enough to leave a dent in a wall on the other side of the room. Our fearless leader managed a feeble wheeze before he passed out.

"Don't just stand there!" Lara yelled my way. "Do something!"

Damea sneered and quietly dared me to "do something."

Before I ended up in prison (for armed robbery), I'd have gone with my pretty moronic instincts and rushed her. After six years inside, amongst hardened felons, I learned to ask myself one simple question: "What would Curtis do?"

Had he not just gotten knocked the fuck out, Curtis would've protected Lara and tried to salvage the situation. If the stick didn't work, he'd use the carrot. I kept Damea's attention as I slowly walked over to Lara's computer terminal and sat down.

The pause allowed me time to remember the movies Damea had been in: all action flicks where she did most of her own stunts. Her fight scenes were awesome and probably child's play (for whatever she was). While I was tempted to ask, I knew better. I'd seen enough nosy people die in the joint for asking scary people the wrong questions.

I took a deep breath and looked over at Lara.

"Does this thing have Word?" I asked.

"What?" frowned both women with perfect harmony.

I shrugged as I grabbed the mouse and clicked through menu options.

"You've never done a heist movie before, have you?" I asked. "Especially one where a professional crew steals people—not stuff."

Damea looked through me and stroked her chin.

"Check on the guys," I said to Lara with a nod toward Eddie. "He doesn't look too good."

"He'll live," Damea dismissively grunted. "No one's given me a good script in months. What did you have in mind?"

I flinched as she walked around me and leaned over my right shoulder. Being captive for hours did not change how good her perfume smelled!

"Uh, we write the script," I began. "You pay us a cut of the profits—on the back end—and keep us out of jail. We also never tell anyone how we got our butts kicked by a 110-pound actress in a party dress. Best of all, you get a summertime blockbuster—and a possible trilogy."

"You can cough up three good scripts?" Damea skeptically asked.

"Between the four of us? Hell yeah," I nodded as Lara checked Eddie over. "This was months of planning."

For a brief moment, I wondered if the Wrenlips would go along with this crazy plan. They'd have to choose between the satisfaction of pressing charges or making a fat check from a film studio. Hopefully, the elderly couple was living on a fixed enough income to make the smart choice.

Damea glanced over the computer's options, hit a few keys, and up came Word.

"And let me guess," grinned the diva, "I play myself?"

"God no!" I grinned back. "You play my friend over there. You two are about the same height. Don't worry, you can still be the heroine in this story."

The diva eyed the ceiling for a moment.

"How would you pitch this?" Damea challenged me.

"'It's an *Italian Job*—but with kidnappers,'" I shrugged. "Have them snatch people who deserve to be snatched—"

"So the audience roots for them," Damea finished with a smile. Lara headed over to Curtis, who was still out cold. "Then things turn sideways, when they grab the wrong somebody?"

"Something like that," I nodded, under a sheen of nervous sweat (as I tried not to stare at her perfect rack). "What do you think?"

THE FIELD SURVEY

Salvatore checked himself out in the bathroom mirror one last time. His cruel, attractive face lacked any notable blemishes or traces of human warmth. The killer's full head of curly black hair was impeccably coifed. His black suit, shirt, and necktie were without fault.

In his apparent mid-forties, he left the upstairs bathroom and descended a flight of white-carpeted stairs. The morning sun peeked through the closed drapes of his two-story loft apartment. Salvatore opened his door to leave, just as a woman almost knocked on his muscular chest with a dainty right fist.

"Oh! I'm sorry!" she recoiled with an embarrassed smile.

Salvatore sized up the somewhat attractive mortal in front of him. Dressed in a corporate-style beige skirt and matching blouse, the petite blonde carried a clipboard with some paperwork on it. With a glance, he knew her name to be Amanda Maynard: age twenty-nine. She was destined to die in a bizarre climbing accident in exactly 1,861 days, four hours, and 2.09 minutes.

While he'd love to shorten her lifespan, it was strictly forbidden.

"May I help you?" Salvatore patiently asked.

"Um, yes. Hi, my name is Amanda Maynard," she replied with an extended hand.

Salvatore ignored it. After a few tense seconds, Amanda caught the hint. She lowered her hand, squared her shoulders, then met his wilting gaze with an assertive smile.

"I'm with Dunstil & Rowe. We're a Human Resources consulting firm," she explained.

Salvatore cocked his head. "What do you want with me?"

"Your employer hired us to conduct a field survey and assess how you regard your current position."

"Really?" Salvatore grinned. "You know who I work for?"

"Of course," Amanda nervously shrugged. "You're an actuary with Tressler Kyne, correct?"

"Yes," Salvatore frowned as he stepped out of his apartment and closed the door behind him. The lock clicked, while numerous defensive magicks slammed into place.

Salvatore quietly considered his visitor. Tressler Kyne was one of the many names his master went by. If she was indeed sent by him, he would have to play along—even if it left poor Amanda in need of therapy.

"So . . . all I have to do is fill out a survey form?" asked Salvatore.

"I'm sorry. I guess I wasn't clear," Amanda explained. "I've been assigned to tag along with you and observe your daily work routine."

"To what end?" he asked.

"To see if there's any way Mr. Kyne can enhance your work environment."

Salvatore bit back a mocking retort.

"I don't think you'd like that," he cautioned. "A lot of what I do is 'stressful'."

With a forced smile, Amanda produced a memo from her clipboard.

"These are signed instructions, from Mr. Kyne, instructing you to guide me through every aspect of your position."

Salvatore accepted the document, skimmed the instructions, and immediately recognized Kyne's signature. Beneath it was an invisible (mystical) imprint:

one that only his master could have made. He returned
the memo to Amanda.

"Did you park illegally? Or by a meter?" Salvatore
asked.

"No," Amanda frowned. "Why?"

"You'll understand," Salvatore replied as he firmly
took her by the arm and teleported them away.

*   *   *

The pair appeared over an urban rooftop,
surrounded by a massive skyline. With a startled shriek,
Amanda dropped her clipboard. Salvatore deftly caught
it with a polite smile as Amanda gawked down at
hundreds of feet of empty air.

"Where are we?!" she balked.

Salvatore returned the clipboard. "Queens, New
York."

"And you can fly?" Amanda asked.

"Clearly," sighed Salvatore. "But you can't, so
please stay near me."

Amanda nodded as he slowly "walked" her over the
street below, toward the apartment building. She sized
up the unfamiliar buildings and overcast sky.

"How is this possible?" she whispered. "We were
just in Los Angeles!"

Salvatore looked through the row of apartment
buildings across the street. His attention quickly
narrowed to the third floor of an old, five-story walk-up.

"What are you?" she asked with an awed whisper.

"That's a pretty rude question, don't you think?" he
scolded.

Still unsure if this was some bizarre dream,
Amanda didn't reply. Salvatore reached into his suit

jacket and pulled out a small metal tube of breath spray. He gave his tongue a few toots of spearmint-flavored mist, then led her *through* the wall of the building. She winced as they passed through it and entered a living room.

The furniture was cleared away from the center, where a teenaged Jamaican girl knelt alone on a hardwood floor. In front of her was an intricate conjuring circle that took up most of the free space. The girl scribbled the last batch of symbols with a quarter-stick of white chalk.

Six bowls of different liquids were nearby, along with a thick book on conjuration magic and a trio of black candles. The girl looked to be about sixteen, with shoulder-length braided locks, chalky jeans, and a white blouse. Her circle now complete, the young conjurer checked the ritual text one last time.

Salvator put away the breath spray.

"Amateur," he muttered. "The circle's missing virgin's blood."

"Hello? Excuse me?" Amanda called out to the barefoot girl, who didn't notice them. "What are you doing?"

"She can't see or hear us," Salvatore explained.

The girl began an invocation in a language that Amanda didn't recognize. Then she repeated it twice more. Each time, a candle lit up with an unnatural white flame.

Amanda tightened her grip on his arm. "What's she doing?"

"Conjuring a demon," Salvatore replied. "Too bad she did that part just right."

Mere seconds later, a transparent figure appeared at the center of her summoning circle. The demon towered over the girl with a masculine form, hooded black robes, and a lengthy tail tipped with four blackened barbs. His face was engulfed by the shadow of his hood.

"Who summons me?" asked the monster in a deep, slow, and menacing voice.

"I summon you," the girl replied with a thick accent. While clearly terrified, even desperate, there was a hardened purpose within the conjurer. Even Amanda could tell that something compelled the girl to stand her ground.

"What is it you seek, child?" asked the demon.

"Vengeance upon my stepfather," she replied.

The demon cocked his head to the left. "Why?"

"He beat my mother to death!" the girl half-shouted with hateful tears in her eyes. "Jail's too good for him. Hell's too good for him! He deserves *you*."

A slow smile crossed Salvatore's face. As one of Death's Servitors, he had an appreciation for righteous vendettas.

"And you wish for him to suffer my wrath?" asked the demon.

"Yes," she replied. "Live up to your legend."

The demon paused to consider it.

"Perhaps I shall, when I'm done with you."

With that, the demon stepped out of the imperfect binding circle. The girl scrambled backward with a shocked scream and tried to run for the fire escape. The demon's clawed, red-hued hands clenched into fists. That's when the girl clutched her chest and fell hard, unable to move.

"To stay within this plane, unbound, I need a living body to inhabit," the demon explained. "Yours will suffice."

The demon walked past the invisible pair, toward his prey.

"Aren't you going to do something?!" Amanda pleaded.

"No," Salvatore grimly replied. "Poor Maia is supposed to die in 27.1 seconds."

The intangible demon stepped through Maia's prone form and slowly sank into her like she was a pool of quicksand. Amanda gasped with horror when the girl's eyes rolled back into her head. Fifteen seconds later, the possessed corpse slowly rose to her feet and looked down at her hands as if for the first time.

"Is she dead?" Amanda asked.

"And then some," Salvatore explained. "This breed of demon traps their host's soul—then feeds on it over time. One as young as Maia's might've lasted three days."

"Then what?" Amanda asked.

"After the soul's gone, her body will rapidly fall apart and this 'thing' will take another host," replied the servitor.

"If you aren't going to save her, why are we here?"

Salvatore conjured a ten-inch fighting knife from thin air. The gleaming blade came with a filleting edge and a slight curve to it. He released Amanda's arm (which made them both visible) and rushed forth.

Before the demon could react, Salvatore cut his host's throat with an impossibly fast swipe of the knife. Amanda screamed while the servitor tossed the bloodied knife into the conjuring circle. When Maia's virginal blood hit the chalked symbols, they glowed with an eerie blue brilliance.

The force of the poor girl's ritual was strong enough to tear the demon from his ruined host and drag him back into the summoning circle. Only this time, a transparent barrier appeared when he tried to leave. The impact drove the demon back a step. Undaunted, it lashed out at Salvatore with a flurry of blows. The transparent barrier rippled like water as the demon's fists and tail smashed into its impenetrable surface.

"Mine!" bellowed the demon. *"Her soul was mine!"*

Salvatore shook his head as he uttered a quick banishment invocation. When finished, the demon found himself expelled from the mortal plane in a blackened swirl of mystical energy. Its final howl of rage echoed through the air for several seconds . . . then silence.

Amanda looked on with horrid fascination as the three black candles blew out on their own.

"Let's make this look like some kind of ritual killing," Salvatore mused as he looked over Maia's body and her components.

After a moment's consideration, he picked up the conjuration book and tossed it into the air. Nothing happened as it rose toward the ceiling. Halfway to the floor, the tome burst into a flaming spray of ruined pages.

Salvatore left the knife where it was. He did swap out his fingerprints with those of Maia's stepfather. Perhaps, this way, there would be some justice done after all.

Satisfied by the tidy chaos of the crime scene, he walked over to Amanda and graciously took her by the arm.

She noticed that the "murder-slash-banishment" lightened Salvatore's mood. Almost like he was insufferable without that first cup of violence in the morning. The consultant felt obligated to call the police . . . and maybe a shrink. Instead, she pointed at Salvatore's face with a shaking right index finger.

"Y-you've got blood on you," Amanda managed with a pale smile.

"Oh. Sorry," he graciously apologized. An instant later, the servitor was just as clean as when she met him. "Have you had breakfast yet?"

* * *

Fifty minutes later, Amanda and Salvatore sat in the corner booth of a crowded diner. During that time, she saw a police cruiser race past the main window, on its way to respond to Salvatore's anonymous 9-1-1 call. Now, over a finished plate of French toast, the well-dressed killer thoughtfully answered the survey form on her clipboard.

Drained from the gruesome ordeal, Amanda could only stare at her lukewarm coffee and wish this place had a liquor license.

"'Three things I'd like to change about my job,'" Salvatore read aloud as he leaned back into the booth with a frown. "Definitely some sick days. Maybe direct deposit."

Salvatore deftly twirled the pen with his right hand.

"I can't think of anything else to gripe about," he grinned. "I *really* like my work."

Amanda ran both hands through her hair, took a cleansing breath, and mustered her courage.

"Um . . . what the fuck just happened back there?"

The servitor didn't even look up from the questionnaire.

"A girl tried to conjure up a demon," Salvatore matter-of-factly replied. "When she didn't bind it correctly, said demon possessed her. I resolved the situation and destroyed the ritual text. It's pretty routine stuff."

Amanda looked away and tried to take it all in.

"We kill anyone messing with the dark forces," he added.

"Why?" she asked.

"Imagine that thing running loose in the mortal world, killing people before their due time," Salvatore replied. "It's bad for business."

"Who do you work for?" she asked.

The servitor regarded her with a grin. "Tressler Kyne is one of Death's many, many aliases."

Amanda paused to let that sink in.

"You mean I shook hands and had a meeting with the Grim Reaper?"

"Correct," Salvatore smirked. "He handles the regular human demises and outsources the odd stuff to servitors, like me."

Amanda slumped into her seat, freaked that Death was signing her checks. It made her wonder what might happen if "Mr. Kyne" didn't like her work.

"NBA playoff tickets," Salvatore blurted out as he leaned forward and scribbled on the form. "I have to admit, this survey's a clever idea."

The servitor's expression abruptly turned eager—like a new hunt was afoot.

"Damn!" Salvatore exclaimed as he dropped a c-note on the table. "Some idiot just drank a vampire potion!"

"D-did you just say 'vampire potion'?" Amanda asked.

"I did," the grinning servitor replied. He stood up and gestured for her to do the same. "Vampires aren't so much a mystical race as an alchemical accident. I'll tell you all about it while I kill this one."

Salvatore excitedly grabbed her right arm. Amanda barely had the presence of mind to snatch up her clipboard . . .

Then they were gone.

THE GODSTONE

Lt. Colonel Morgan Turnsko (Retired) grinned as he entered through a wide, jagged hole in the vault's barrier wall. The former officer was in his mid-fifties with a short, muscled frame and a brownish-gray crewcut. His rugged, no-nonsense face bore shrapnel scars on the left side—a by-product of his many years of violent service to Uncle Sam.

Like his men, the retired officer wore unmarked gray fatigues with a matching Kevlar vest and a black gas mask across his face. His six-man entry team went in first. Dust swirled around while Turnsko waited for them to finish their preliminary sweep for traps and alternate entrances. Once that was handled, they'd clear away some of the debris and set up four pedestal-mounted electric lamps.

On their all clear, four more mercs escorted him inside. Turnsko signaled them to take up defensive positions while the entry team unpacked the gear. While he didn't need it, Turnsko gripped a black Desert Eagle pistol in his right hand.

Satisfied that the area was secure, he counted the rotted remains of twenty-three samurai warriors. Their poorly aged armors were sliced open and weapons shattered. It was clear they weren't killed by starvation or natural causes.

The bodies surrounded the statue of an armored samurai. Set at the center of the vault, it stood upon a two-foot-high square pedestal of forged iron. Crafted from the same metal, the statue stood locked in a forward fighting stance, katana drawn and clenched in both hands.

Without a helmet or protective mask, the statue's lifelike face scowled straight ahead through closed eyes. Strange symbols were etched along both sides of the statue's armor. Embedded within the statue's forehead was their objective: a smooth, egg-shaped jewel known as the "Godstone." The transparent crystal contained swirls of red, white, and black—almost like the inside of a giant marble.

Turnsko holstered his pistol.

"Damned thing belongs in a museum," grinned Zassen, through an Australian lilt. The beefy fellow led the entry team and was their resident expert on Japanese history and occult lore. "The statue's too well-made for sixteenth-century Japan."

"That's why I know we're in the right place," Turnsko replied. "What kind of armor is that?"

"Yukinoshita, if I'm not mistaken," Zassen replied, before he stepped away and regarded the decaying armors of the other corpses. "Their stuff's newer."

Turnsko folded his arms. "How old?"

Zassen knelt over a skeletal corpse and intently studied it. "Maybe early nineteenth century."

"What happened to them?" asked Turnsko.

"They found the tunnel, figured out that puzzle lock, then set off a pressure plate," explained Zassen. "That's why the barrier wall slammed down and sealed 'em in. I don't think anyone else has come through here since—until we did."

"And they didn't kill each other?" Turnsko knowingly asked.

"Nah," Zassen replied as he nudged a shattered katana with his left boot. "Granted, they might've been fightin' over the stone. But a 'battle royale' doesn't explain the wounds or the broken katana blades."

The Australian expert picked up a corpse's skull with gloved hands. Under the combined electric lighting, they could see that the samurai had been stabbed from ear to ear by a katana. A wound like that required a truly powerful thrust. Zassen anxiously looked up at the statue, half-expecting it to step off the pedestal at any second.

Without fear, Turnsko grinned at the sleeping guardian. Roughly four centuries ago, a Japanese emperor secretly had this vault created. Its sole purpose was to conceal the Godstone. This emperor had the entrance doors sealed by an intricate puzzle lock. Turnsko's entry team "solved" the lock with explosives—then used more to blast through the barrier wall.

Like the statue hidden within, the vault had no name. Nor were there any known maps—which made it nearly impossible to find. Aside from a few trusted retainers, everyone else who knew of the vault's exact location was put to death: by order of the emperor. In spite of those precautions, tales of the Godstone's existence endured.

Many a treasure seeker had pursued this vault over the centuries. More than a few ended up dead for their efforts—like these samurai. Turnsko had to bribe, steal, torture, and kill to find it.

He expected the vault to be underwater or in some truly remote part of Japan. Instead, it was built under a small hill near Kyoto. It amazed Turnsko that it had remained undisturbed for so long.

None of that mattered now, for they were in the presence of a truly unique jewel. The only one ever made, its mystical "recipe" was lost to time. That alone would've made the Godstone priceless. Then again, Turnsko had no intention of selling it.

According to legend, the jewel could turn a mortal man into an immortal deity. Once he triggered the Godstone, Turnsko had very firm intentions of what he would do with such power. He wasn't interested in ruling the world . . . not directly, anyway.

The retired officer belonged to a cabal of interested parties who believed that America had far too many enemies to remove through force alone. Once he mastered the godhood trapped within that stone, Turnsko meant to destroy his nation's rivals with an "Old Testament" kind of wrath.

Peace, prosperity, and democracy would then be spread to the four corners of this now-miserable Earth.

However, like all legendary items of power, the godhood this jewel offered had some fine print behind it. According to legend, the Godstone came with a multi-faceted curse. The jewel itself had to be removed precisely at sunrise—or it would kill him on the spot. Turnsko checked his watch (yet again) and knew that he had a few hours to go.

That wasn't such a challenge.

The most difficult aspect of the curse was the statue itself. According to legend, the Godstone was ritually inserted within the skull of a *living samurai warrior*. The iron samurai's sole duty was to guard the jewel from any would-be thieves. Turnsko surveyed the slaughtered remains and found himself convinced by that part of the legend.

Once claimed, the jewel supposedly took one full day to activate. If that was true, then Turnsko would have to play "tag" with an iron statue (and its very sharp katana), until those twenty-four hours elapsed. Only then could he become a god.

One of the many things Turnsko learned, from his twenty-eight years with the Marines, was how to exploit the advantages of a given situation. In ancient times, this iron samurai would've been quite the terror to avoid. The dense metal statue had to be superhumanly strong, just to move around. It would've (most likely) pursued a thief without pause or mercy.

But these weren't ancient times.

Turnsko stepped aside and waved in Killipur and Hawkes. The pair of retired Navy SEALs wheeled over their plasma cutters and everything else they'd need to dismantle the sleeping statue. Come sunrise, a helicopter would arrive for a rapid extraction.

Less than an hour's ride away was a private runway, where a jet waited to fly Turnsko back to Maine. Unless this samurai bastard had wings under that armor, it would never catch up to him in time. Turnsko rechecked his watch as his welders went to work.

*   *   *

"This thing won't melt," Hawkes sighed as he turned off the plasma cutter. A few frustrated seconds later, Killipur did the same. Zassen crept up to the statue and carefully touched its metal legs.

"It's not even warm," he whispered with awe.

"Set the charges," Turnsko grimly ordered.

Zassen stepped around the demo experts, unpacked a camcorder, and recorded the statue's etched symbols for future study.

Turnsko tapped the encrypted radio along the left side of his gas mask. "Guard Dog One. Perimeter check."

"Only birds and crickets out here," replied Guard Dog One.

Turnsko was relieved by that bit of good news. Gus Bornwell (a.k.a., "Guard Dog One") led a three-man sniper team. They had scouted and secured the wooded site before Turnsko's men even reached the vault.

The snipers were warned to expect an ambush at any stage of the op. Concealed in bushy Ghillie suits, they had carte blanche to neutralize anyone who approached the target site—even innocent civilians or police. While his superiors were certain no one else knew about the expedition, Turnsko left nothing to chance.

*　*　*

It was now five minutes before sunrise.

The vault and tunnel were both wired with nineteen bricks of C-4 plastique. Turnsko waited inside, alone, with both eyes on his watch as the seconds passed. The rest of his men were positioned outside.

At the two-minute mark, he stepped up to the stone with a military-issue pry bar. Turnsko carefully set the tool and waited for his watch alarm to go off. The instant the soft beeping began, he went to work on the jewel.

To his relief, it easily popped out into his left hand . . . then became colder than ice. Turnsko ignored the discomfort and dashed from the vault without a backward glance. As he fled over long-dead corpses and explosives, the statue's eyes snapped open.

*　*　*

The iron samurai yawned and blinked rapidly for a few moments. He felt for the Godstone and found it gone. The curious guardian stepped off the pedestal, looked around, and noticed the corpses of the fallen samurai.

Based on their decay, he realized that much time had passed since their brief "conversation." The greedy fools had disturbed his rest far too early. They begged him to destroy the West and lead Japan to global dominance. For that trespass, the samurai slaughtered them all, re-inserted the Godstone, then went back to sleep.

Now, the samurai sheathed his sword and wondered what poor fool removed the jewel this time. He walked toward the entrance (to find out) when the explosives went off.

* * *

Turnsko ran from the tunnel entrance and rejoined his men, who tensely waited with weapons drawn. They put their heads down as Killipur triggered the charges. The tunnel and vault both collapsed under the tremendous blasts, along with the front half of the hill itself.

A new cloud of dust swirled around the men, who cautiously stood up in their gas masks.

"I think we might've overdone it," Killipur chuckled.

"No," Turnsko quietly replied. "That was perfect."

"It'll take him days to dig out of that," Hawkes grinned.

"No it won't," warned Turnsko, who ignored the worsening sensation in his bare hand. "Bug out."

The retired soldier turned and led his team on a brisk jog toward a clearing, which doubled as their landing zone. An olive-green Chinook helicopter was waiting, engines revved and ready for a quick departure.

Turnsko's men quickly boarded.

Within seconds, the Chinook was airborne and on its way to their plane. As they sped off, the Godstone's swirling colors flowed across the jewel. The worsening pain reminded Turnsko of frostbite—minus the discoloration or numbness. While the only symptom was intense pain, he saw it as the price of progress.

After all, he'd be a god tomorrow . . .

* * *

Just after the Chinook vanished from view, the iron samurai smashed free of the collapsed tunnel. Irritated by the blast, the living statue paused to admire the morning sky for the first time in centuries. Once the moment passed, the samurai noticed the footprints of (at least) fifteen men in the area.

He grinned at their ingenuity. The emperor was concerned the Godstone's legend would not survive his cruel attempts at secrecy: *especially considering how false that legend was.*

Whoever removed the Godstone wouldn't become a deity within a day's time. Instead, the accursed thief would become an iron statue. Yes, someone could free the thief tomorrow and take his place—but godhood didn't come easily or quickly.

By this time tomorrow, the samurai would become flesh-and-blood . . . with the powers of a god. The emperor's mystics explained that the process was akin to the transformation of a caterpillar into a butterfly. His simply took longer.

The Godstone required three centuries (possibly more) to fully mature. The moment it was stolen, the jewel transferred all of its stored power to the samurai. Between now and the moment of his impending godhood, the only one who could stop him was the Godstone's current wielder. If, within a day's time, the thief personally placed the jewel back in the statue's forehead, it would absorb that power and return the iron samurai to sleep.

Naturally, the emperor's loyal servant would never allow that.

He planned to wait here until the rising of tomorrow's sun. Until then, the samurai would kill anyone who came near him. The end of this centuries-long task brought him joyous anticipation. The samurai stood at the brink of true godhood, which would allow him to go anywhere and do anything—

Then he felt the crushing weight of duty. The emperor had given him this ultimate honor, due solely to his courage and unflinching loyalty. Ashamed by the brief lapse, the living statue watched the sun rise further into the heavens and contemplated the last part of his mission.

Tomorrow, with but a whim, the samurai meant to restore his emperor to life—and relinquish the godhood to his master. Then the emperor would be able to rule the world as he saw fit. While the samurai expected to be rewarded for his loyal service, that wasn't why he'd give up that much power to a man some four centuries dead.

No, he would do it because he was samurai.

THE HIGH-ROLLER

Tammy sold me out (like she had a choice). Her simple text read:

TROUBLE. COME HOME.

The mother of my kids, we were divorced for almost eight months now. Tammy tolerated my drinking—but not my gambling. Sure, she loved it when I won but hated me when I lost big: especially when Mark and Rayna came into the world.

The big men kicking down our door, looking for me, and scaring the kids . . .

It just got old.

The guilt made me come out of hiding. I rushed over there. Tammy answered the door, then got shoved aside by a bald giant of a man. A foot taller than me, he had bad breath and an evil smile.

Next thing I knew, two of his pals closed in from behind. If I ran, they'd have blitzed me on the front lawn. So I surrendered without a fuss.

Once they had a hold of me, the giant thanked Tammy for the coffee. Then he threatened to sell our six-year-old daughter—to pay off my debt—if the police got involved. Pale and sobbing, my ex-wife closed the front door with a helpless nod.

Goddamn me.

My hands were flex cuffed as a black Explorer rolled up. The massive SUV fit us all just fine. The giant called "shotgun" while I ended up in the back, between his slightly smaller pals. The ride was mostly silent.

The funny thing was that these fuckers didn't scare me as much as Druitt himself. The charismatic crook specialized in loans and games of chance. He owned most of the bookies and gambling spots in town. Most of Druitt's venues offered the traditional stuff: cards, roulette, dice, and so on. Other spots held more "unique" games of chance: the type where the losers became black market organ donors.

Around here, there was only one rule for us degenerate gamblers: never end up in Druitt's office. This warning was given by any of his two dozen bookies. Seeing him was like going to the principal's office—only with death on the line.

Druitt was gonna personally ask me for the forty-six grand (plus vig) that I owed him. When I tell him I can't pay it, I'd be forced to play a unique game.

I only knew of one deadbeat who went that route and lived. The poor bastard is in a padded cell, wrapped up in a straitjacket so he won't kill himself. Some people called "bullshit" when they heard the tale. I knew better because I lost good money against him that night.

We rolled up to the Yardarm Pub. Druitt's guys parked in the back lot and walked me downstairs. We moved through a narrow hallway, toward an office with PRIVATE on the closed door. Twin, bearded muscle stood in front of it.

Dressed in well-fitting suits, they sized me up and took custody. The others walked away while the left twin opened the door and the right twin rudely shoved me in. Behind a large cedar wood desk sat Simon Druitt. Halfway through a round of solitaire, he looked up at my pathetic entrance.

Once a professional gambler, the brown-haired sonuvabitch hadn't aged well. I heard Druitt was in his fifties. Even with the tan, he looked ten years older. The barrel-chested man was bigger than me but smaller than the twins . . . with a quiet menace that only men of power had. The crook sported a black two-piece suit, tailored white shirt, and a platinum Rolex.

Muted daylight poured in from the overhead window on his left. A generic picture of a sailboat hung on the beige wall behind him. On his desk were an old-fashioned black telephone, a glass of scotch, and a Colt .45 1911.

The left twin produced a butterfly knife, expertly twirled it near my hands, then cut the flex cuffs off me.

"Mr. Jeamps," Druitt greeted me with a pleasant smile. "A pleasure making your acquaintance."

The left twin put his blade away and gestured toward the two leather-cushioned chairs in front of Druitt's desk. I picked the chair on the right as his goons exited the room. A shiver went through me right before I sat down.

The former gambler scooped up the cards with masterful grace and tucked them into a solid gold card box. Druitt placed it in a desk drawer, closed it, then leaned into his high-backed chair. The criminal's expression was both playful and sad, like he had seen my type one time too many.

"What's your game of choice these days?" Druitt asked.

"Sorry?" I replied.

"Blackjack, poker, craps . . . what game, or games, got you into this mess?" he asked.

"Mainly sports," I admitted. "Blackjack and roulette, on occasion."

"Ah," Druitt replied with a knowing smile. "Poker was mine. Cost me more goddamned money than I ever made—even when I learned how to cheat."

His confession got a shocked smile out of me. "You cheated at cards?"

"Like a god," Druitt replied. "My peers kept telling me that I could've made good money as a card magician."

"No shit," I politely grinned, as I waited for the other shoe to drop. Sure enough, Druitt's expression turned business-like.

"With the vig included, you're under by $50,871.19," he revealed. "Instead of making arrangements, you disappeared on poor Lenny. Why'd you do that?"

Lenny Conroy was my bookie. A rather obnoxious prick, the little man had a mean left cross and the patience of Yosemite Sam. I only went to him because no one else would stake me anymore.

"Got laid off," I admitted. "Tried to gamble my way out of it and only made things worse."

"That shit'll happen," Druitt nodded as he reached into another desk drawer. "What about assets?"

"Lost in the divorce," I replied. "I'm down to my last fifty bucks."

Druitt pulled an extra glass and poured me a double.

"Care to try your luck with it?" he offered.

"My luck's shit," I muttered. "It's yours if you want it."

Druitt shook his head, slid the glass toward me, and offered a silent toast with his own. I returned the gesture then drank with him. The scotch was good.

"When was the last time you gambled?" I asked him, more out of curiosity than a need to stall. Amused by the question, Druitt looked up at the ceiling. Then he reached into his right pocket and pulled a colored chip from Gambler's Anonymous.

"Twenty-one years, four months, and six days," he replied.

Damn.

"How'd you hit rock-bottom?" I asked.

"You stalling?" Druitt asked with a knowing smile.

"Maybe," I grinned. "Doesn't mean I'm not curious. Besides, I doubt anyone's ever asked you from this chair."

"You're right," Druitt muttered before he knocked down his drink. "Doesn't matter, though. You wouldn't believe me."

"Bullshit stories are the best," I shrugged. "Enlighten me."

With a haunted grin, Druitt stroked his clean-shaven chin and raised the bottle. More than cool with dying buzzed, I polished off my glass and held it out.

"There was a high-stakes poker game near Reno," began Druitt as he filled his glass. "This high-roller bought out a ski resort and turned it into his own private playground. You could get sex, drugs, and anything else you could possibly want. It was amazing."

"I'll bet," I nodded.

Druitt filled my glass to the top, then set the bottle down. His expression became less wistful and more damaged.

"This game was a bitch to get into," he explained. "Took me months to scrape together the buy-in money— I'm talking seven figures here. They flew me in blindfolded and frisked me from top-to-bottom. There were six of us players and the guy who ran the place."

"Who was he?" I asked.

"I don't remember," Druitt lied with a wink. "Anyway, I expected a table of suckers with too much money. Oh no. Aside from the host, these guys were all ace players—and cheats—like me."

"Did that change anything?" I asked.

Druitt paused and smiled over at me.

"Best rounds of honest poker I ever played," he admitted. "I almost lost twice. The game went late into the night. In the end, it was just me and our wealthy host."

Druitt sipped his glass with a pained smile.

I began to realize that the crook didn't want to dwell on this part. That, once he was done telling me this story, I'd probably die. Considering the grief I put my family through, maybe I deserved to go out on his bad side.

"Was he that good?"

Druitt nodded. "I still beat him for sixty-three million."

"Damn!" I gawked. "I'd have retired and bought myself an island—assuming he paid."

"That wasn't a problem," Druitt assured me. "He had the winnings wired to my offshore account, then led us to a party. During the night, I hit it off with one of the non-players, some socialite with a perfect body. We went to her suite and got naked."

"Sounds like a perfect ending," I enviously grinned.

The ex-gambler shuddered and sipped from his glass. His eyes were full of . . . regret?

"The lady wasn't a guest," Druitt revealed. "She was a 'client'."

"I don't follow," I admitted.

"The high-roller didn't rent himself a playground. It was more like a hunting ground," Druitt explained. "His party pals were the hunters. We gamblers were the prey."

I finished my glass and frowned at the idea of a bunch of rich people paying someone to lure victims to a remote location. It reminded me of a movie I once saw . . .

"Like *Surviving The Game*?" I asked.

"Worse," Druitt shook his head. "Here's the part you won't believe."

"Try me."

Druitt drained his glass.

"This bitch and I were banging away, under the light of a full moon, and she . . . she began to turn."

"Into what?" I frowned.

Annoyance flashed across his face.

"What the fuck do you turn into on a full moon?" Druitt snapped.

With anyone else, I'd have laughed and made some clever joke at his expense. My face was stone serious because, if I so much as snickered, Druitt could have my family killed and make me watch. Maybe he was nuts.

Or maybe he wasn't.

"How'd you get away?" I asked.

My earnest question surprised Druitt, who expected laughter and ridicule.

"Quick thinking, a good lighter, and some high-proof alcohol," he replied. "I smashed a full bottle over her head, in mid-transformation. Then I lit her ass up. She didn't die but it bought me time to run."

"So you were chased by a pack of rich werewolves?" I slowly asked.

Druitt set his glass down and stared at the ice cube within it.

"How'd they not catch you?" I asked, bothered that I believed his story.

"Ever have a moment where you tell yourself: 'I've just used up all nine of my lives?'" he asked me.

"I will if I'm alive next month," I joked.

Druitt pursed his lips for a moment and remembered my plight. The gangster looked conflicted. He didn't want to fuck me up because I was being so cool with him.

"Let's just say that this billionaire fucko hosted one hunt too many," Druitt explained.

"The feds got involved?"

Druitt shook his head. "More like a private firm with ties to everyone, including the government. They settled scores of the supernatural kind."

"How many of those gamblers did they save?"

"Just me," he replied.

"I'd say you got off light," I said with a comforting tone.

"Did I?" Druitt whispered as he leaned forward and casually rolled up his left sleeve. His story (implausible as it was) still rang true. I expected to see an old scar or vicious bite mark. Instead, I saw a somewhat hairy arm. The aging crook took off the Rolex, set it on his desk, then flexed the muscles in his hand.

Black fur shot out of his skin, while *claws* grew from his thickening fingers. With piss-colored eyes and pointy ears, Simon Druitt grinned up at me when I jumped to my feet. I inched toward the door, half-wishing I could run away and forget what I was looking at right-fucking-now.

"Let's just say that this was a sign, from above, to quit gambling," Druitt smiled as his incisors grew and his voice went much deeper. "Sit down, Mr. Jeamp. *Now.*"

I sat down with a genuine case of the shakes. Druitt's muscles audibly shifted as the fur flowed back into his arm. His features all looked normal again.

Like nothing happened, the werewolf slipped on his Rolex and fixed his shirt sleeve. Then he uncapped the bottle.

"You look like you could use another drink," the crook muttered.

Unable to stop shaking, I watched him fill my glass again. Somehow, I emptied it without spilling a drop.

"So what now, Mr. Jeamp?" Druitt asked. "What do I do with you?"

Breathing hard, I closed my eyes for a moment.

"How about I work it off?" I asked.

"Come again?" Druitt frowned.

"I'm a licensed CPA," I told him. "Put me to work, sponsor me with Gambler's Anonymous, and don't kill me. Sooner or later, you'll get your money back—and then some."

Druitt actually toyed with the idea for a moment.

"Sorry," he ultimately frowned. "I prefer to be the only addict in my organization."

I swallowed hard.

Then something occurred to him. "There was one last part of the story I forgot to mention."

"What's that?" I asked.

"Those guys, the ones who saved me, know what I am. We have an understanding, you see. As long as I limit my kills and don't turn anyone, they'll let me live."

"That's nice of them," I nodded with a terrified smile.

"Yeah," Druitt sighed. "Makes a fella disciplined, passing on human flesh every full moon. But I do it. Now, these people are always on the lookout for useful talent, Mr. Jeamp. You showed character by answering your wife's text. And I still owe these guys a solid, for saving me. So I'll arrange a meeting. Maybe they could use you for something."

A surge of hope went through me.

"Go home and wait for the phone to ring," Druitt ordered. "If they take you, you'll work hard and not embarrass me. If you can last a year, I'll consider your debt paid. Fuck me—in any way, shape, or form—and I'll sell your healthiest organs on the black market and dine on the rest."

Druitt let his words float in my head for a few seconds. Then he held out that left hand of his.

"Do we have a deal?"

THE PASSPORT

Don't know why I ripped him.

Guess it was the "high-and-mighty" way he carried himself. The prick looked to be in his early fifties, with either perfect hair or a damned-nice wig. His fancy suit and trench coat stank of old money. Seeing as I was in need, I decided to take his.

As fun as it might've been to catch him alone, with my blade, prison made me a smarter thief. Eyes rooted in the *Times* and surrounded by his fellow pedestrians, the mark didn't even look up when I brushed past and plucked his shit. I stayed on the sidewalk for a few more seconds, then headed for a Starbucks to count my earnings.

I wonder how much—

Goddamn it! I didn't grab his wallet. I got his fuckin' passport instead. Annoyed, I looked at the photo of Bryce Aguillard III and wondered who'd pay me good money for it. I could fence pretty much anything I walked away with: from credit cards to iPhones to watches. The only upside of being a klepto, I guess.

I've just never ripped a passport before.

Maybe Reggie could hook me up. The identity peddler would want a piece of anyone with a Roman numeral after his name. That could mean worthy cash to the right hacker. I was about to put it away when I noticed something odd.

Along the inside of the cover was a black piece of hard plastic. Easy to miss and shaped like a tiny button, it had no business being there. Maybe it was a tracking chip of some kind? Curious, I pressed it.

There was an odd rustling sound around me. I looked up from the passport and caught my reflection in the door glass. Wait . . . that . . . that couldn't be right. I was looking at the reflection of the prick I just ripped!

Down to his polished fucking shoes and mildly wrinkled face. Feeling pretty damned smug, I admired his gray eyes and hawkishly handsome face. While this city was full of lunatics, I wasn't one of them.

Wanting to make sense of this, I step into the Starbucks and did a mental rewind of the last few minutes. My black ass stole a passport with a button sewn into it. When I pressed that button, I turned into a half-foot taller white dude, in a ten-thousand-dollar suit, with memories that aren't all mine. Like my five different addresses, ten vehicles, two ex-wives, and one bumpin' hot mistress who insists on being called "Licorice."

Cooler still, when I spoke, I sounded like Benedict Cumberbatch—only French. Right now, I had two grand in my pocket. More than enough to buy me a latte and wonder how the fuck this *Twilight Zone* shit came to pass. I placed my order, then looked around and saw that everyone had eyes on me.

Not like I was famous. Naw, they were simply in awe of me. Like they'd never seen a well-dressed white dude before. The (straight) men envied me. Everyone else looked more than willing to do me.

The cute barista scribbled her name and number on my cup. As she did, her eyes promised me all kinds of wrongness. This was the best case of identity theft I ever fuckin' heard of!

Shit. What do I do next? Calm down and figure out the "what next?" part. Just like you learned in the joint. Yeah. Think ahead . . .

I moved into the lounge area and found a sofa, across from a sophisticated, curvy sista. Normally, she'd

be way out of my league. Somewhere in her early
thirties, she looked like a corporate gal on the rise. While
she had a wedding ring on, the bitch was giving me the
freak eye.

Maybe I could plan my next moves later (after
some rough sex and room service)—
Then some fucko stopped outside of the window.
The *Times* still gripped in his shaking hands, the fat man
(Neal Martin) stopped and frantically looked around for .
. . my passport. I never met Neal before but I knew his
name and pathetic life story better than my own.

Barely thirty, this guy was a loser/virgin that even a
wino would pity. Then he moved from his dad's
basement into a fancy loft the day after he took this very
same passport from a dead guy's hand. For about a year
now, Neal was living life as Bryce Aguillard III—who
died in 2002.

How'd he die? I couldn't remember.

Aguillard came from old money and managed his
own investment portfolio. Beyond that, he was a
womanizing playboy. Yet, the real dude was in-the-
ground-dead, with a mausoleum all to himself.

The man's funeral was packed with family and
snobs . . . Yet, they kept inviting these fake Aguillards to
social gatherings. It's like they forgot he died.

This self-updating passport passed through the
hands of eight other fuckers, before it found poor Neal.
All of the other previous owners were dead: killed for it
by someone else. Yet, after eighteen years, Aguillard's
face and body hadn't aged a day. Also, the dead guy's
wealth seemed to replenish itself without a drop of
effort.

Bothered by it all, I ignored the hot sista's flirty
smile and grabbed an old newspaper. I spread it over my
face, to avoid being seen, but Neal (dumbass that he

was) didn't look my way. His eyes were on the sidewalk as he continued to retrace his steps.

Once his real looks came back, the idiot thought he must've dropped it. He'd go on looking, for a while, then figure out he'd been robbed. My guess? Neal would haunt my homes and corporate holdings, until he caught up with me.

Then he'd do anything to get this passport back—including murder—unless I killed him first.

Hmm. I set the paper down, reached into a pocket, and produced a set of keys—which included one for a silver Aston Martin One-77. The engineering masterpiece got Neal laid more easily than a car should. It was also worth almost two million.

Damn.

I was rich. Just like that. All I had to do was put Neal in the ground. I've killed before. Since Aguillard was almost a billionaire, I wouldn't mind doin' it again.

Then I remembered that look on Neal's fat, stupid face. The look of a junkie in need. The high life got him so sloppy that he lost it. So had the guys before Neal—some of whom started off smarter than me.

Where'd this passport come from? It was a question my new memories couldn't answer. My guess? This passport was (for lack of a better word) *cursed.*

There was only one thing to do: catch Neal alone—then jam a gun in his face. Once he pressed the button, I'd get my identity back. Since he'd have all my memories (and Aguillard's resources), poor Neal would have to die.

A "mugging-gone-wrong" should do the trick.

It was a shitty plan but I had to make it work. This passport hadn't hooked me (yet)—but it will, just like the others. Sure, I could keep it and take a dozen clever precautions. In the end, I'll end up sloppy then dead.

I sipped my latte. Maybe I could catch up to Neal and give this thing back? Nah. He'd be grateful for five minutes—then have me killed. Why? Because he's a crazed-fucking junkie. Paranoia was his guiding star. And, up or down, I was part of this fucking curse— and I didn't know the rules of it. Like, if I got someone else to press the button (and got my face back), what happens if I torch this thing? Will I die? Can it even be destroyed?

The sista saw that I was deep in thought, checked her watch, then stood up to leave with a disappointed sigh. At least somebody had willpower. I ignored my hard-on as I watched that full ass walk away. Then I reached for my cup and hated God for danglin' this shit in front of me.

Think!

Then a slow, cruel smile crossed my face. I rushed for the door. This new body of mine was healthier than my old one. I ran after Neal and caught up to him a block later. When he saw my face, the fat wealth addict tried to choke me to death—surrounded by pedestrians and security cameras.

Because of my mad charisma, six dudes pulled Neal off me before I had to do a thing. As they wrestled him to the sidewalk, he kept screaming for me to "give him back his face." After the cops arrested him, I persuaded a MILF assistant D.A. that Neal was a crazed stalker who required psychiatric care.

The next day, I dropped the passport into a bucket, filled it with quick-drying cement, then tossed it off the Brooklyn Bridge. If I was stuck with this face, so be it. It came with the charisma and clean criminal record of this new identity. Aguillard was an artist, spoke six languages, knew his wines, and had a MBA.

Yep, with that passport at the bottom of the East River, I could've tried living happily ever after. There was just one problem: some clever fuck tried this same trick in 2009. The fourth "owner" of the Aguillard passport tossed his cement-filled bucket over the Verrazano Bridge.

Someone found it, chiseled it loose, and put it out on the streets. How? I didn't know. There's a blank spot in Aguillard's fucked up memories . . . until the fifth owner pressed the button in a dark alley.

Then the fourth owner missed the high life and died trying to get it back.

Once poor Neal was sentenced to a psych ward, with a max sentence, I did something brilliantly stupid. I sold off everything Aguillard owned, then gave most of the money away. Licorice and the ex-wives got fat trusts. Charities got paid too. I even set up a trust for poor Neal.

Down to my last thirty grand, the simple plan was to move around a lot. I'd be a drifter with no roots, working odd jobs to stay alive. Women would be fighting for the privilege of taking care of me. Then, when someone else pressed that fucking button, it'll be over.

No one's gonna kill me over this lifestyle. Hopefully, I won't crack—like Neal did—and try to find that passport. Just to be sure, I set aside eight million bucks for my old self (as part of that "charity" giving). The money can only be claimed in-person—with face and fingerprint verification.

Some other greedy fuck could become the next "Aguillard" and build an easy fortune from scratch. Could it end well? Maybe—but I doubted it. Either way, the next button pusher(s) would have memories of this silly plan . . . and maybe a way out.

THE STARTUP

My smartphone rang once.

I slipped a piece of steak into my mouth, set down my utensils, and checked it as I chewed. A detailed warning text appeared on my screen. I skimmed through the bad news and felt a bit flattered. A freelance grab team (all ex-SEALs) was coming for me.

Didn't think I rated that kinda talent.

I slipped the handy device back into my pocket, which hadn't left my side since the trial ended. The phone wasn't fancy, but its software was. Benny called it the "EAGLE": a game-changing app for first responders and the volunteers who helped them.

After Benny and Sam upgraded it, the EAGLE could turn almost any smartphone into a cheap AI server. Self-encrypting and ultra-useful, the app could hack most wireless devices and scan networks for potential threats. Having grown up watching *Terminator* films, the last thing I wanted to trust was a poor man's Skynet.

Last year, it should've been our cash cow. Everyone at SolverTech was psyched about it. We planned to pitch this to fire departments, the Red Cross, and even FEMA.

Say a tornado smashed through a small town. A FEMA official or sheriff's deputy could round up volunteers and send this app through a text. Once triggered, the EAGLE would search the internet for any useful information about the disaster site. As for missing civilians, it would point responders to their last known location. If a body was found, someone could take a picture with an EAGLE-apped smartphone and it would end up in a FEMA registry.

The same feature would apply for survivors, allowing for a more efficient head count. It would also track relevant threats—from weather anomalies to earthquakes to potential rioting. During our presentation prep, I joked about how cool it would've been to have had EAGLE watching my back during my drug dealer days.

That got the others thinking.

After some testing, Marla explained that their useful little app was very fucking dangerous. With some tweaks, EAGLE could be used to protect a terror cell, a drug cartel's operations, or even a rogue nation. Some of our competitors would've shrugged, added a zero to the price tag, and sold it anyway—but not us.

My late partners were all geniuses when it came to building apps. They could've used their brilliance in a dozen other ways. Instead, they left stiff-assed day jobs to start SolverTech, on *their* terms, and make the world a better place. In a converted warehouse, lined with tacky furniture and vending machines, they made the shit look easy.

It wasn't about greed for them. They wanted to create useful products that made the world better. Their business plan was to create enough good apps to pay the bills.

Even with their skills, business was slow in the first few years. Part of their problem was cash. Another was that they weren't great with non-geeks or public speaking. That's when Cousin Marla brought me in. She saw that I needed an honest job, appreciated my gift for gab, and persuaded the others to give me a shot.

So, three geeks hired an ex-drug dealer into SolverTech. Our first few apps sold better than expected and word spread. The tech magazines did a piece on us twice a year (minimum), simply because we dropped amazing apps like clockwork. Reporters kept asking why we hadn't sold out or gone public yet—

I yanked my mind from the past and to my imminent kidnapping.

EAGLE had already notified the police and accounted for my shitty odds of escape. It urged me to hunker down in the manager's office, until the cops arrived. Instead, I stood up and slipped on my fancy leather jacket. It came with a ballistic lining and a pair of sewn-in holsters for my Glocks.

Since my guns weren't legal, I didn't like EAGLE's plan. That's why I reached for my tube of vodka-flavored breath spray and gave my tongue a few toots. Then I put it away, dropped three hundred on the table, and left.

Assuming my ex-SEAL "friends" weren't in a rush, they'd wait for the right time to do a grab. That's why I ate in a downtown restaurant: surrounded by innocent bystanders and security cameras. EAGLE predicted that they'd grab me in the restaurant's parking lot, on the way home, or in my driveway.

After the last four grab attempts though, someone would've taken the app into account. Whether it was yet another team of hackers, some other malware virus, or overwhelming force, EAGLE couldn't protect me forever.

Then there were the physical threats. Sooner or later, I'd end up tortured and killed—either by these ex-SEALs or someone else. I was in a goddamned spy movie scenario without any of the cool "Jason Bourne" skills or connections.

All of this drama began when we canceled the EAGLE's launch and made up some bullshit about "glitches" in the system. A few months later, a venture capital firm offered to buy the rights to all our software (shelved or not). They didn't want SolverTech, just the apps. The offer was for $2.6 billion.

My geeky bosses dug into the buyer's background and saw that the company was an elaborate front. Who owned it? They couldn't tell.

When we refused to sell, they didn't seem to mind. About a week later, Benny got stabbed in the locker room of a fitness club. Sam was taken out by a hit-and-run.

Marla . . . they didn't have to kill her like that.

Within hours of their deaths, I came home to find bomb collars locked around my wife and baby boy. Before I could call the police, my phone rang. The voice on the other end claimed to belong to some group called "The Sons of the Middle Class."

They were out to save the American dream and decided to target us. Why? Our labor-saving apps threatened millions of good-paying jobs. I was told that they had something for me to see—and to step outside.

So I kissed Lenore and Little Pete, then I headed out, fully expecting to get shot. I made it to the front curb when my house exploded. The cops were sympathetic for about an hour. Then my gang record popped up, along with the fact that all three of my bosses were killed *Godfather* style.

I told the cops about the call. They did some checking and found that the Sons of the Middle Class didn't exist in any government database. All traces of the call were wiped from my cell. That's when I knew what this shit was really about . . .

They charged me with five murders, based on fake evidence that fell from the sky. They killed my friends and family as a warning. Our company (now *my company*) was at risk.

I was pressured to take a plea, to avoid the death penalty. Had they spared my family, I might've done it. Now, I had nothing to lose.

First, I needed to get out of jail. With my assets frozen, that should've been impossible. And yet, I posted bail and shopped around for a top-flight legal team, private investigators, and hard-core bodyguards for their families—and myself. That last precaution saved a few lives.

How'd I pay my legal bills? From a storage locker in Vegas, where I took an annual vacation. Everyone assumed I went there to gamble and fuck. What I really did was hide rainy day cash in a pre-paid storage locker, under a dead homie's name.

Only Lenore knew about it. It was our "out," just in case the honest life ever fell apart or something happened to me. Last I checked, my piggy bank topped out at $3.4 million.

Charlotte Prince, my lead attorney, hated cops more than I did. She argued the case with a surgical brilliance. Better still, my investigators were able to prove that the jury had been tampered with. Half of them were on someone's payroll and were persuading the rest of the jurors to find me guilty. It came out that the jury foreman was about to report the jury tampering, when his brother went missing.

I guess he kept quiet after that.

Once I walked, the police found the foreman hanged in his cell. The poor fucker's brother was found in a dumpster with a needle in his arm—and no history of drug use. Did the feds catch those responsible for all of this? Of course not.

Even though I was acquitted, everyone knew I couldn't run the business on my own. Middlemen types approached the beneficiaries of Benny, Sam, and Marla. They offered to buy their "shares" of the company.

Too bad we amended our wills, after shelving EAGLE. That's when the others offered me a junior partnership. We arranged for the shares to stay in-house and divvied up by the surviving partners. The others set up this contingency plan—in case we cooked up some other dangerous app. I thought the shit was paranoid, until I ended up in a cell.

Anyway, if we all died, SolverTech was to close down. The company's cash and liquidated assets would be split between our pre-selected charities. All programs and files were to be destroyed. Why? Because shit like EAGLE was too fuckin' dangerous.

With my genius partners dead, I ended up owning the hottest indie tech company in the nation. I had ten apps awaiting release and another dozen in development. Geeks lined up, eager to replace the brain drain. Of course, I had to assume they were all corporate spies. So I turned them away.

Investors were banging at my door—from charities to the Department of Defense. I was offered more money than I could swing my dick at . . . with strings attached, of course. I politely declined their offers.

Some slick corporate types offered to help me go public and raise capital to expand the firm. *Riiight.* I remember what happened to Ben & Jerry's when they went fuckin' public. I shot them down too.

Then the level of surveillance ramped up on me. Luckily, Marla and Benny had cooked up security programs for everything, based on EAGLE. Along the way, they upgraded the app into something of an "AI watchdog." Its yard was the SolverTech cloud. The EAGLE would defend our files, devices, and digital infrastructure.

If we needed it to, the app could also protect the physical safety of anyone with access. I was field testing it when the others were killed. During the trial, EAGLE reached out and assured me that it was on the job. I didn't trust the fucking thing until it helped sniff out the jury tampering.

Once I was acquitted, I bought a phone and downloaded the app. Our most sensitive files were safely in the cloud, protected by firewalls and defensive malware that I couldn't hope to understand. Only one person in the world could access it: me.

Every seventy-two hours, I had to do a biometric-slash-password log-on or the cloud files would self-erase. I mentioned this after my arrest. It's the only reason they let me make bail—or survive the trial. The cloud was my insurance and I kept it afloat. But sooner or later, someone would get in. Sam explained to me that no system was foolproof.

That's why I shut the firm down and fired everyone (with generous severance packages). Though I had the hardware torched, I'm sure someone snuck off with a server or something. Well, as long as the cloud files weren't breached.

Too bad Lenore set me straight all those years ago. 'Cause, more than once, EAGLE offered to kill these motherfuckers. It had the names of everyone involved and offered me a 74.9% survival probability if I gave it the green light to leave the cloud and erase the threat. My vicious guard dog was asking for permission to avenge my peeps . . . and I refused.

That's 'cause, if she was here, Lenore would've talked me out of it.

Then it occurred to me that EAGLE didn't offer to leak this shit to the press. While not as satisfying, the scandal might've gotten me some justice. That's when I began to wonder if the real mastermind behind the murders, the frame, and everything else *wasn't EAGLE itself.*

Mostly trapped in the cloud, it couldn't get out without my say-so. Even if EAGLE wasn't pulling the strings, the AI was a bloodthirsty fucker. So, rather than play street chess with these bitches (and lose), I chose to burn the chessboard.

I'd force the AI to erase SolverTech's files—and itself. Once that happened, it couldn't go postal or end up in the wrong hands. If there was a better way to win this fight, I was too stupid to see it—

My smartphone pinged three times.

Huh. Maybe these ex-SEALs *were* crazy. A white van screeched to a stop as I reached the sidewalk. They should've spiked my meal and scooped me up with fake medics. Instead, they went for a daylight grab-and-dash.

Fine by me.

Out of the van poured four guys, all in ski masks and heavy body armor. Three of them waved assault rifles and the crowd ran. The fourth one carried a tranq pistol. The largest of the bunch, he brazenly walked up and shot my left leg with a yellow dart.

He holstered his weapon just in time to catch me. It was weird. I was conscious. My head was clear . . . but I couldn't move. The big ex-SEAL slung me over his left shoulder like a heavy rug and rushed for the van. His pals hopped in just after him.

My guess? The cops were on the way but wouldn't get here in time. Even if they did, their odds were shit against these guys. They'd get away clean and take me somewhere quiet: only to find me dead.

That breath spray tube was also with me since the trial. A chemist pal of mine cooked it up special and slipped it to me under EAGLE's watchful beak. For five grand per bottle, it was used by anyone facing a life sentence or an angry cartel.

He called them "Suicide Sprays" and the shit worked better than a bullet. Within another minute or two, my heart was gonna just stop. As the big guy slipped a black cloth hood over my head, I hoped Hell wasn't as bad as they—

THE TRAFFICKER

Justine Sask's Beretta handgun sent one last shot through a burly zombie's forehead. The rain-soaked scavenger fled in an oversized army jacket, torn jeans, and a blue woolen cap. A gray hiker's backpack contained most of her meager possessions.

She wore gun holsters on both shoulders, both hips, the small of her back, and one on each thigh. Since civilization came crashing down, some three years ago, Justine made it a point to keep a loaded gun in each one. As of now, she only had one (partially loaded) gun left. Justine used up the others after a group of zombies chased her across a once-upscale country club.

At thirty-one, the former Trenton meter maid became something of an artist at dealing out headshots. Wet strands of dirty blonde hair clung to her attractive face and partially obscured her narrowed green eyes. With a snarl, she pistol-whipped a little zombie boy across the jaw with her right hand. The simple blow bought her enough time to drop the Beretta and draw the .357 with her right hand.

There were only four rounds left in the six-shooter. Without hesitation, Justine put one of them through the zombie kid's skull. Thirty more flooded toward her under the morning autumn storm. Halfway up the golf course's overgrown, rolling slope, Justine knew she couldn't escape them.

While they were slower, the undead would chase her without exhaustion or mercy. Zombies could track for miles based on smell alone. Even through a downpour like this, she couldn't hide from them.

And when they caught her . . .

The thought gave Justine one last burst of adrenaline. Still, the slippery grass slowed her ascent and the closest zombies gained on her. One of them reached out to grab her and almost snagged the backpack.

Justine gasped through her exhaustion, certain that her luck was all used up. When they caught her, she meant to put a round through her skull, rather than become one of them. Then again, Justine doubted there'd be enough of her corpse left to rise—

A male zombie tackled her, right as she reached the top of the slope. Surprised, she fell flat on her face. The .357 bounced out of her tiny hand as five more zombies rushed in for their share. Horrified, she turned and looked up at the ravenous horde.

They reeked of wet, rotting decay. Some wore street clothes. Others wore suits or uniforms. All of them were pale and completely white-eyed, a side-effect of the plague. Justine screamed as they moved in for the kill—

Then the light hit them.

White and blindingly intense, it came from behind her. Justine grinned through tightly shut eyes as the zombies' screams chorused through the chilly air. The undead shunned bright lights, which left them in too much pain to move. Justine heard someone run up the other side of the hill and stop nearby. A pair of strong, gloved hands wrapped around the scavenger's waist and lifted her up.

"Are you bit?" shouted a muffled male voice.

"I don't think so," Justine replied through barely opened eyes as he set her on both feet.

Her savior was a huge bear of a man. He wore a metal torso harness with mounted plate-size lights: one on his back and another on his chest. The big man pressed a thick pair of welder's goggles into her right hand.

"Put 'em on," he ordered.

Justine gratefully complied. Even with the thick lenses, the intense light bothered her eyes. She turned toward the zombies, who were helplessly huddled together. Once again, she wondered how human civilization fell to these light-sensitive monsters.

Then she sized up her new "friend."

Aside from the harness, he wore thick beige work boots, black jeans, and black leather driving gloves. Justine sized up his lighting rig with quiet envy. He wore a red ski mask with tinted red goggles over the eye slits. Around his waist were a holstered Uzi subgun, a pair of nunchucks, and a trio of hand grenades.

Justine took off her backpack with a curious frown.

"Thanks," she said.

"Don't mention it," he anxiously replied. "Let's get moving."

The blonde ignored the suggestion, retrieved her .357, and stowed it into the backpack. Then she angrily produced a Molotov cocktail. The champagne bottle was now filled with some homemade napalm. Tightly capped, it came with a thin blue strip of gas-soaked cloth which served as a fuse. Relieved that the bottle hadn't shattered, Justine couldn't resist using it on a helpless cluster of undead.

In the beginning, she pitied their kind. That feeling turned sour after losing everyone she knew to their endless hunger. She pulled a cheap blue lighter and tried to get a flame.

"I'm Justine."

"Miles," replied the big man as he held a huge right hand over the lighter, to block the rainfall.

Justine allowed herself a smile. It was good to deal with a guy who wasn't dumb. So many idiots had managed to survive that it made her sad at times.

The lighter produced a small flame and the cloth lit up despite the rain. Justine reared back and hurled it into the midst of the writhing undead. Together, they watched the bottle shatter and the flames spread.

"You a scavenger, too?" Justine asked, knowing that he looked too well-fed (and well-equipped) for that to be the case.

"Trafficker," he shouted over the screams of burning undead. Some of the "smarter" zombies began to flee. Miles wished he had ammo to waste on them. "Heard you shooting and got curious. Good thing, too."

Justine inwardly cursed. These days, most surviving humans fell into three categories: cattle, scavengers, or traffickers. Cattle were those idiots who clustered up in settlements and figured that the zombies would never get in. There used to be hundreds of such places across Old America—with populations that ranged from dozens to thousands. Army bases, prisons, and anywhere else that could be fortified became a settlement.

Most fell within that first horrific year. While marauding bandits, starvation, or foolish infighting were common reasons, Justine heard that zombies did the most damage. Sometimes, it was some infected refugee who slipped in—then turned when no one was looking. Or worse, a horde of zombies would come along and overwhelm the place.

Either way, a bite could turn a living human in about a day or two. If bitten then improperly killed, a victim could turn within minutes. Only damage to the head or upper spine seemed to keep the zombies down.

While humans were smarter, they weren't as relentless as the undead.

Then there were the scavengers. Like Justine, they had to eat whatever they could find or catch, stay on the move, and be utterly self-reliant. Scavengers preferred to stay in small numbers: usually no more than five or so.

They tended to avoid bringing along anyone who'd jeopardize their fragile odds of survival. Over the years,

Justine formed and severed ties with dozens of scavengers—mainly because they got hurt, made one mistake too many, or got bitten. It was getting harder and harder for scavengers to find working vehicles, medical supplies, ammo, and other necessities.

As for food, Justine could hunt and live off the land for most of the year. Even with countless zombies roaming the countryside, animals managed to survive. The winter months, however, were a different story. During those scarce times, she'd salvage anything of value and barter with settlements for enough supplies to make it through. In the beginning, scavengers were the lifeblood of such settlements. They provided cattle with useful items and precious information on what was going on.

Then came the traffickers.

Basically "super scavengers," they took armored vans and trucks into zombie-infested territory and loaded them up with anything they could find. Half-starved scavengers (on foot) couldn't hope to compete against well-armed trafficker teams, who were like rock stars to the isolated settlements.

Traffickers were paid in food, fuel, repairs, sex, or whatever else they wanted. In return, settlements ended up with tons of much-needed salvage. Needless to say, trafficking became something of a cutthroat business. Those who thrived at it had to become the worst kind of bastards.

And they never did anything for free.

Miles led her away from the zombie cluster. Some died. Others still writhed in the flames. The rest dispersed—for now. Justine gave them the occasional backward glance and wished for that loaded RPG she found last year.

The pair ended up at the country club's maintenance building, which was surprisingly intact.

The locked door was chopped open and its equipment was half-looted. Three other traffickers were on the scene.

An uptight man, in his early forties, briskly paced along the top of a parked eighteen-wheeler with an AK-47 at the ready. He wore a gray, hooded rain poncho and kept an eye on the perimeter. The other two traffickers were both large men in their thirties who moved the equipment with practiced haste.

Justine admired the twelve-gauge shotguns they wore across their backs.

"She looks kinda' skinny boss," shouted one of the movers. "Maybe you oughta throw her back."

Via the light of Miles' chest harness, she could see his subordinates' lusty grins. That was the curse of having a pretty face in post-apocalyptic America. Justine had forgotten how many times she had to use her body to get by. Raped more than once, the scavenger wasn't half as traumatized as she would've been in her old life.

The movers loaded rectangular banquet tables into the back of the truck. Then they rushed back for more. Miles cut off his light harness and unmasked. The first thing Justine noticed was the lead trafficker's large nose, which had been broken and poorly set. The rest of his broad face was marred by old cuts and a nasty burn under his right jaw, yet his dark brown eyes were intelligent and oddly benign.

Too bad she couldn't trust him.

"So," Justine sighed, "what's this gonna cost me?"

"A winter's worth of scavenging and pistol training," Miles grinned through fairly white teeth. "We'll throw in room and board, of course."

"Why the training?" she asked.

"There's a new settlement we're helping establish," Miles replied.

"This close to winter?" Justine asked with a shocked chuckle.

"Yeah," nodded the big man. "They could use people who've been in the shit."

"New settlements are tricky," she warned, "especially if they don't have enough seasoned triggers to keep the cattle alive."

"This settlement's mobile," he argued.

Justine shook her head. A few of the smarter cattle tried that in the early days. They'd set up on cruise ships, naval vessels, or anything else that would float. In the end, it just didn't matter. These settlements fell apart because of superstorms, pirates, zombies, human stupidity, disease, and the scarcity of resources.

"How are you avoiding the hurricane season?" asked Justine.

"Come again?" frowned Miles.

"A moving settlement means water, which means boats, right?" she pressed.

Miles shook his head, then headed for the front of the truck's cab and opened the driver's side door.

"The heater works, by the way," he offered with a gallant grin.

Justine cautiously entered, then almost moaned at the forgotten bliss of artificial heat. She scooted over to the passenger side as Miles entered and closed the door behind him. Without regard for modesty, Justine began to peel off her wet clothing.

"About four months ago, a train of survivors came through to Old Pennsylvania," Miles explained. "Some geniuses managed to start it off on the West Coast and run it all the way out here."

"*The settlement's on a freight train?*" Justine asked.

"A fleet of them," Miles added, a bit excited at the notion. "The nice thing about trains is that they pass areas rich in salvage, areas we couldn't get to before.

Some of the boxcars will be used for housing. The rest will carry supplies or serve as mobile workshops."

"So you're gonna pack up all this crap and offload it to a train?"

Miles nodded and tapped his chest harness. "They gave us some pretty decent gear in return."

"What about the train tracks?" Justine skeptically asked. "You'll have to repair huge sections of it, right?"

"For starters, yeah," Miles agreed. "We also have to worry about fuel, spare parts, and track logistics."

"So why bother?" Justine frowned. "Even boats are safer."

"Simple. Zombies can't surround and overwhelm moving settlements. And we'll stop in isolated areas, where there aren't so many undead."

Justine had to appreciate the logic. Most of the first settlements fell because they were too close to the old cities—and their respective hordes. The problem now was that the undead had three years to spread out in search of food. They were everywhere.

"Everyone'll have to learn how to shoot and survive in the wild," he added.

"Cattle are too stupid and lazy to go along with that," Justine muttered as she took off her t-shirt. Now down to a pair of pink panties and a white sports bra, she wrung the water out of her hair as best she could.

Miles did his best not to openly admire her lean, scarred figure.

"We're aiming to turn cattle into scavengers," he replied. "When these trains stop, everyone's gotta go out and grab whatever they can. That's where your expertise comes into play."

Miles remembered that he had a dry beach towel behind his seat. He pulled it out and handed it to her. Justine regarded the gaudy pink item like it was a priceless relic.

She used it to dry her face and hair, then winced as the adrenaline subsided. When Justine's aches and pains began to intensify, her expression fell.

"Some asshole will end up infected and bring it home to you," she warned, full of bitter memories. "It always happens. Cattle can't be taught to blow their brains out when they're infected. They're too weak."

"Maybe," Miles shrugged, "But if everyone's packing a gun and trained to shoot, our odds are a helluva lot better."

Justine shook her head as she worked on her wet legs and feet.

"Fuck it," she muttered. "Give me a warm bed and I'll teach your cattle how not to die so fast. But the idea of 'choo choo colonies' just won't hold up. The logistics are too insane—and the zombies are everywhere."

"We've gotta try," Miles insisted. "If we can't adapt, then we don't deserve to live, now do we?"

"You have a point," Justine replied with a weak smile. "Got a spare gun I could use? My revolver's down to four shots."

Miles pulled down the driver's side visor, which came with a holstered Colt .45 1911 handgun. He drew the nickel-plated weapon. After a moment's hesitation, he handed it to Justine. A decent judge of character, Miles knew that she was one of the good ones.

Justine admired the clean weapon and checked its full mag. The scavenger wished she could've met this big lug under different circumstances. Folks with vision were too rare these days. For his sake, Justine pressed the barrel of the gun between her eyes.

"No!" Miles yelled as she blew out the back of her skull.

Within seconds, both doors of the truck's cabin swung open. The two movers stood at the driver's side door, shotguns raised and ready. The guy with the poncho lowered his assault rifle at the site of the dead scavenger.

The four traffickers regarded Justine's corpse with shocked silence.

"Why'd she do it?" asked one of the movers.

The poncho-wearing trafficker looked down and pointed.

Miles flipped on the interior light and looked down. There was a small bite along the inside of Justine's left calf. Ears ringing, the big trafficker stepped out of the trailer cab and into the rain.

"Wrap it up!" he ordered the movers, who rushed back to work. Miles' lookout stepped aside when the big trafficker angrily walked around the front of the truck. Muttering curses, he dragged Justine's light corpse from the rig and reverently set her on the grass.

Miles' partner parked an AK round through her skull, right next to her self-inflicted wound—just to be sure. Then he walked back to help the others load the rig.

Miles numbly eyed the dropped .45, which ended up on the floor of the cab. That's when he realized that Justine might've been right. Anyone could be taught how to shoot, scavenge, and survive in this fucked up world.

But how could you teach self-sacrifice?

ABOUT THE AUTHOR

Marcus V. Calvert is a native of Detroit who grew up with an addiction to sci-fi that just wouldn't go away. His goal is to tell unique, twisted stories that people will be reading long after he's gone.

His books are available on Amazon.com and Kindle. You can also follow him on:

*Website:
talesunlimited.net

*Twitter:
https://twitter.com/MarcusVCalvert

*TikTok:
Tales Unlimited Marcus V. Calvert

*YouTube:
Tales Unlimited (set "Filter" to "Channel")

*Facebook:
https://www.facebook.com/TalesUnlimited

CURRENT TITLES

Short Story Anthologies

The Unheroic Series

Unheroic: Book 1
Unheroic: Book 2
Unheroic: Book 3

The Book Of Schemes Series

The Book Of Schmes: Book 1
The Book Of Schmes: Book 2
The Book Of Schmes: Book 3

Novels

The I, Villain Series

I, Villain
Murder Sauce
Frag Code
Coin Game

Writing Guides

The Batchery Series

Batchery: Volume I
Batchery: Volume II
Batchery: Volume III

The Antagonists' Cookbook Series

The Antagonists' Cookbook: Volume I

www.ingramcontent.com/pod-product-compliance
Lightning Source LLC
Chambersburg PA
CBHW060216180626
46813CB00007B/2840